The Beautiful Dismal Woods

Short Stories From the Adirondacks

Ryan Schmit

Troy, Ohio

The Beautiful Dismal Woods: Short Stories From the Adirondacks is a Clay Bridges Communications & Publishing publication.

Requests for information, copyright permissions, or comments should be addressed to: Clay Bridges Communications & Publishing, 300 South Ridge Avenue, Troy, Ohio 45373 or info@claybridges.com.

Edited by: Kate Johnsen
Cover Design by: Brandon Haskins
Interior Design by: Melissa Leembruggen

Clay Bridges seeks to provide resources and education to build up people to span life's circumstances. For speaking, training, publishing, or author events, please visit our website at www.claybridges.com or contact us at the information listed above.

Library of Congress Control Number: 2010931116
ISBN: 978-0-9819807-6-8

Printed and Manufactured in the United States of America

the
beautiful
dismal
woods

stories from
the adirondacks

ryan schmit

[Table of Contents]

[This book is dedicated to]

The Adirondack Mountains are filled with intriguing names from Native American languages. The title of this work, *The Beautiful Dismal Woods,* is derived from "Couchsachraga," the English translation of the Iroquois word meaning "dismal wilderness." The Couchsachraga mountain peak is one of the locations in this collection. While the area is named "dismal wilderness," it is indeed a lonely, dangerous, and breathtaking element of nature to experience and is therefore a beautiful dismal woods.

Chapter One

[A Letter Home]

Dear Son and Daughter-in-law,

I hope this letter gets to you in enough time, for the approaching storm is very dangerous, and you'll need to take the necessary precautions at home in Old Forge.

Your mother and I had a very interesting weekend with this storm, which started as I was driving home from work last Friday night. The weatherman on the radio said a severe winter storm was approaching our region, and a winter storm warning had been put into effect through the weekend. I didn't think much about the approaching storm, since I'd seen a few flakes in my lifetime, but when I got home your mother was watching the news as usual, and the TV station was having live coverage around the region.

They even had one reporter standing in front of a Department Of Transportation salt building, and he said, "They are using bulldozers to put salt into the dump trucks." (In my opinion they're using front-end-loaders and snow-plows, but maybe I'm wrong, and that's what they call them in this part of the country.)

After the news report was over, your mother said she was really worried that we might get snowed in, and we should stock up on groceries. Well, we got bundled up in our winter clothes, and I drove your mother into town. By the time we arrived at that newfangled general store, a few flakes were already falling. I tell you, it was a madhouse. Everyone who was anyone was there. The entire store was packed, and all of the shelves that had contained food were now bare. Everyone was grabbing food, batteries, salt, and even snow shovels left and right. I couldn't believe everyone was panicking about this approaching storm; it was just a few flakes. Even your mother was scared because she couldn't get a gallon of milk for breakfast, but she won a fight with a young woman trying to grab the last box of oatmeal. I think if I had stood still long enough in one place someone would have thought that I was a mannequin, and people would have started stripping my clothes and buying them for themselves. We got out of that crazy general store by the skin of our teeth with some of the groceries that your mother needed for the next week. Hopefully, the store would restock and stay open all weekend long.

Well, when we left the general store, it was snowing something awful fierce. It was a whiteout. I couldn't see no further than a mile, and everyone was all over the road. I had a difficult time staying on the road with all of the cars spinning out and going into ditches. There were lots of unfortunate accidents all the way home, but luckily my driving skills got your mother and me home safely with our precious cargo of food.

Once home, I turned on the TV, and watched the weatherman. The temperature was going to fall to record lows as the snow piled up. I told your mother that we should stoke the furnace good and put on our long johns because this house was going to be cold before morning. I could hear the whipping winds howl, and I thought the roof was going to come off during the hearty supper that your mother cooked for me. We went to bed early, wearing long johns under our nightclothes, and your mother added two quilts to the bed. The only problem we had during the night was that we roasted ourselves and had to strip off one of the quilts.

We got up early Saturday morning, and your loving mother told me to get the newspaper out of the mailbox. I said, "Considering how much wind and snow there was last night, I don't think the paper could have been delivered this morning. All the roads are probably closed with drifting snow, and the plows must be having a difficult time keeping the main roads open since I haven't heard a plow go by the house yet."

Your mother still insisted that I go out and get the paper, so I changed out of my nightclothes, leaving my long johns on, and into a pair of jeans and a flannel shirt. Your mother got out my winter jacket and snow pants from the closet, while I put on my wool socks and winter boots, hat, and gloves. When I was fully dressed, I went to the garage, got my snowshoes down from the rafters, and strapped them on. Hearing the wind still blowing just as hard as last night, I tied a rope from the bumper of the car to my waist just for safety's sake. Hanging on the wall was my ice ax, which I grabbed just before I opened the door and was blown back until I regained my balance. The snow had drifted to the height of the doorknob, and I climbed over the drifted snow to head out into the unknown.

Once I was outside, all I could see was a beautiful white blanket of fresh snow. Though, of course, I was in a whiteout and could barely see my hand in front of my face. I took out my compass from my jacket pocket to properly determine what direction I should head. Breaking a new trail was difficult at best, but this was nothing that I hadn't done before. I was just worried that my tracks would fill in before my return trip. As I turned the corner of the house I felt the sting of the blowing snow hitting my exposed face, and my breath was taken away by the cold wind blowing right through me.

I estimated a headwind of nearly forty miles an hour with gusts over sixty, and at those speeds the wind chill was nearly fifty below. It was slow going as I used my ice ax for balance but almost fell backwards twice from the gusts. I really didn't want to be blown back to the garage door and have to restart my expedition for the essential morning newspaper. After making slow progress toward the mailbox, I started the climb toward the road. Even with the crampons on the bottom of the snowshoes, for every step I took forward, I slid back a half a step. Being out this long in the wind and cold, I could feel my fingers and nose starting to freeze. I knew I had only minutes to get back before my extremities started to get frostbitten.

As I neared the top of the ascent, I could finally see the mailbox sticking out of the snowdrift. The mailbox post was completely buried in snow. With a few steps left, the combination of steep terrain and sheer wind speed threw me off balance. I fell down and started to slide. Luckily, I turned over on to my back and dug my ice ax into the snow, slowing my descent until I finally came to a rest at the base of the climb. I rested there for a few minutes; the top of the snow pile blocked most of the wind. When my strength returned, I decided to head back up the slope for one last try at getting this morning's paper. Turning over, I released the bindings on my snowshoes and started to crawl toward the crest of the snow pile. I struggled toward the mailbox on hands and knees. When I reached the box, I used the ice ax to dig out the door and opened it.

The newspaper hadn't been delivered this morning, and I started to feel a sinking feeling for my wasted effort and risking my life. I knew your mother was wrong in thinking a newspaper deliverer would risk their own life to deliver a meaningless paper. Shaking my head in disappointment, I closed the mailbox door and headed back down the slope to retrieve my snowshoes. After refastening the snowshoes, I noticed my tracks had disappeared in the windblown snow. I looked at my compass, and it was frozen solid and useless as the wind-driven snow around me. In desperation I started to struggle in the snow, trying to find any trace of my tracks until a tug at my waist reminded me that I had tied a safety line to the bumper of my car. I pulled the rope tight and followed it back to the garage door that was almost filled in by snow. I was able to clear enough snow from the entrance to slip inside the garage. It took a few long minutes to close the door with the forcefully blowing snow piling up on the floor, but with my last ounce of strength the door was shut, if for nothing more than to save my wife and keep her from sacrificing my life for her reading pleasure.

After regaining my strength again, I stripped my outer layer of clothing and headed into the house ready for a steaming cup of coffee to warm my frozen body and mind. I shouted to your mother as I entered the kitchen, "There won't be a paper delivered this morning." Your mother was sitting quietly at the kitchen table and eating her bowl of oatmeal when she finally asked me about the weather. I told her about my expedition and near death in the wintery wasteland beyond the garage as I made myself a bowl of oatmeal and a cup of coffee.

As I sat down at the kitchen table, your mother with a bleeding heart said, "I didn't know how dangerous the weather was going to be, and how you would risk your life for something that didn't arrive this morning. I can only feel ashamed of myself for being so self-centered and not caring about the one who I love so dearly. That's all I can think about now as I read the comics." She pulled today's paper from her lap and began to read the local weather on the front page with a grin across her face. "Cold and clear with three to six inches on the ground from overnight and a slight breeze from the north."

I was flabbergasted that your mother had risked her life and had gone outside in her robe and slippers to retrieve the newspaper while I was getting prepared for my expedition to the mailbox. Your mother is now reading the comics and won't give me any section of the paper until I have written you about my life-threatening expedition.

    Love,

    Your Father

P.S. The reporters are saying that this was one of the worst storms in Dayton history. I don't know what they would do if they got a normal day's snowfall from back home. Maybe give up on life and freeze to death?

Chapter Two

[Mud]

I told the waiter, "Mud! If I see another speck of mud, it'll only be too soon." He just nodded my way and walked off.

Journal, you might ask, "Why do I hate mud so much?" And I'd reply with a calm, smiling demeanor, "It's not that I hate mud. Mud is just mud. When it's left to itself, mud doesn't see, smell, taste, hear, or feel anything. It's inert, harmless, inanimate, unexciting. It's a pool of dirty water." But that response doesn't answer your question, and you would have to ask it again.

I would think for a few moments, look straight into your eyes, breathe in deeply, and step back to build up my courage to answer your question. Then all at once I'd yell at the top of my lungs, "It's because I abhor mud! It's filthy, smelly, gritty, squishy, and slippery. All of my adult life I've lived in the finest and cleanest New York City apartments money could buy. The apartments were cleaned at least once a day by my maid, but I'd spend hours scrutinizing every inch, overseeing their work, making sure they didn't miss anything, including the crumbs. I changed my clothes several times a day just because I perspired in them. They were washed immediately. I always got into my spotless car in my white and spotless underground parking lot just to avoid the dirty city air. I've sold cars not because of mileage or wear, but because of the thinning paint or an impossible stain. I've not only lived in the cleanest apartments, worn the cleanest clothes, and driven the cleanest cars money could buy, but I've also tried to live the cleanest of lives so that I don't get sick."

But your question would still not be answered. Why do I abhor mud? Well, it's not any old mud, mind you. It's not the everyday gritty mud found in a street puddle, or even the squishy mud from a freshly watered lawn that I hate. The mud I'm talking about makes mud pies look runny. The best description I've ever heard describes this mud to be thicker than the richest chocolate pudding New York City has to offer.

The mud I'm talking about has its very own name: Adirondack Boot-Sucking Mud. You might pause and think for a moment before asking the next question. "How did Adirondack Boot-Sucking Mud and a New York City clean freak ever come near one another?"

"Well, Journal, let me tell you my story."

Two of my best friends in the whole world, who shall remain nameless (Mr. Everett and Mrs. Olivia Tremper), have described to me their numerous adventures up North. They've gone on and on about the clean, quiet, and peaceful environment of the Adirondacks, where for over an entire century the richest and most famous people of New York City have spent their summers vacationing. They have talked of it as one of the cleanest, most serene, and beautiful spots in the entire world. My two friends have invited me on numerous camping trips, but I've passed up on each opportunity until now.

After nagging me like forever, Everett asked me again one dreary fall day in the City, "Allen, you've got to go camping with us this weekend. The leaves will be at their peak; the weather will be perfect; and there is definitely no better time than now."

I replied with my usual reply, "I don't have any camping gear. Believe me, I don't have a clue what I would need or even how to camp, therefore I'm not going."

"Don't worry, we've got extra stuff for you to use. We'll bring everything for you: food, clothes, sleeping gear, et cetera. You'll have the best time of your life! It will be fun." A pause. "I know you love looking out over Central Park when the leaves change, but where we're going, it's a million times better. Come on just once, have a little adventure. Stop being as stiff as your collars! Live a little."

This time I knew Everett and Olivia just wouldn't take no for an answer, so I finally had no choice and agreed to go with them.

At the god-awful hour of five in the morning, they dragged me out of bed and threw me into the back of their black H2 which had two boats strapped on top. The back of the Hummer was loaded with packs and paddles. After riding half the day, we finally stopped in a gravel parking area surrounded by woods with a small dirt ramp leading toward the shore of Hoel Pond.

We all got out and stretched our tired muscles. My knees were so stiff and achy I had trouble walking to the water's edge, where I saw numerous cottages along the eastern shoreline. The pond, if you could call it that, for it was at least three city blocks to the opposite shore, had very small waves lapping up the boat ramp. The northern and western shorelines were covered in a blaze of vivid reds, oranges, and yellows while a cumulus cloud moved out of the sun's way. Green pines broke through the expansive canopy, muting the overall canvas, but the few mountains that rose above the trees were impressive. I stood motionless to properly absorb the breathtaking views, knowing that City views could never really compare with what I was seeing now.

At the back of the Hummer, Everett and Olivia loosened the ropes holding the thirteen-foot and seventeen-foot carbon fiber canoes that were still on the roof. Everett and Olivia are the sweetest couple any person could have as friends, considering they brought everything for this three-day camping trip. Everett was born somewhere in the Adirondacks 58 years ago, grew up here until he went to college for a business degree, and finally ended up on Wall Street. He met Olivia one day over spilled coffee. She spilled it on him, and it was love at first sight. Having been married for thirty-plus years, his salt and pepper hair still catches Olivia's green eyes every now and again. It seemed strange to see Everett in clothes other than a long-sleeved shirt and tie, but he did look ruggedly good in his

L.L. Bean wardrobe, dark blue crewneck, tan slacks, ankle-high Gore-Tex hiking boots, and his New York Mets cap. A pair of wraparound shades hid his clean-shaven face.

Olivia stands on her tiptoes to kiss her husband on the lips. Her slender body still looks as good as the day they met, even after raising three children. She also was adorned in L.L. Bean clothing, a red turtleneck and tan twill pants with a pair of Gore-Tex hiking boots. Her wraparound shades were hanging from a band around her neck. Her long straight black hair flowed gently in the breeze from the pond.

"So, where is the camp?" I asked.

"It's four ponds over, about a four-mile canoe trip," Everett replied.

Everett and Olivia expertly removed the smaller canoe from the top of their H2 and walked it toward the shoreline. They returned, and I helped Everett unload the second canoe, placing it next to the other.

Olivia opened the back of the Hummer and started to remove the packs and paddles. I asked if I could help, but they declined and insisted that I look through all of my equipment and get changed. I was given a dark red backpack. I opened it up and found a green sleeping bag with a plaid pillow, a compressed bedroll, and two empty bottles for water.

I commented, "Must be pretty hard beds we're sleeping on tonight."

Everett replied, "Somewhat."

In the back seat of the H2 I replaced my white gym shoes with my new pair of two-tone colored hiking boots and put on a down-filled red jacket to keep the autumn coolness away. I brought all of my essentials: changes of clothes, toothpaste, razor, shaving lotion, and enough biodegradable toilet paper to last me a week in the wilderness. I had even brought enough bottled water for the weekend because you never know when Montezuma will choose to get his revenge. After I crammed everything in the pack,

I struggled under the weight to carry it down to the dock, where Olivia secured it into the canoe.

When Everett locked the Hummer, he asked me, "Ready to go canoeing?"

Not knowing much about canoeing, I cautiously nodded my head and said, "I guess so."

Since Everett was an expert canoeist, he got stuck in the smaller canoe that carried all of the camping gear.

Olivia sat at the water's edge with the stern between her legs and said to me, "Get in the front of the canoe."

With all but the stern in the water I stepped onto the bottom of the canoe. The boat started to rock back and forth, and I became very unbalanced, almost falling into the water.

"Crawl forward before you tip the canoe," Olivia said while struggling to keep the canoe upright. I did as she asked. Slowly and carefully I crawled up to the bow seat and sat down.

"You should turn around so you can help paddle," Everett said.

"Oh, O.K." I replied as I swung my legs around.

Before I was even settled, Olivia pushed the canoe into the water. The canoe scraped bottom until it reached deeper water. With two splashing steps Olivia jumped into the canoe, and we were propelled forward into the pond. The canoe rocked back and forth until Olivia settled into her seat, and we smoothly glided out into the pond. A few seconds later Everett's canoe scraped bottom, and I saw him jump gracefully into the back of his canoe.

Being only a few inches from the surface gave me a different perspective on the water. Having only been on yachts and ferries, which allowed me to walk anywhere, I was not accustomed to a canoe, where the slightest motion would start it rocking back and forth.

Everett guided the two canoes northwest to a point across the wide pond. I tried my hand at paddling and was extremely surprised at how well Olivia could adjust to my erratic paddling. She kept us on a straight course.

Thirty minutes later we arrived at our destination, which was an old railroad embankment with a three-foot diameter drainage pipe running underneath. As we neared the shoreline, Olivia said, "Allen, carefully jump out, grab the canoe, and climb up the shore. Do you remember how I was holding the canoe when you got in?"

"Yeah," I replied.

"Do the same for me as I get out," she replied.

I looked out at the shoreline in front of me and told Olivia, "The shore is covered in way too much mud. Can we move over a bit?"

Olivia back-paddled and moved the canoe a few yards to the right where the stones reached the shore. I climbed carefully out of the boat, turned around to pull the canoe onto shore, and held it for Olivia. Everett ran his canoe onto shore and got out without anybody's help.

After taking a water break and studying the descent flow through the pipe, Everett said, "I will send the canoes through the pipe. You two catch them on the other side."

Not knowing what to do, I climbed up over the tracks with Olivia and could see the pond that lay before us. Olivia climbed down the other side to the pipe exit and waited for the canoes to float through. I was amazed by the view of Turtle Pond, but broke from my silent reverie when Olivia yelled, "Get down here and grab the line when I catch the first canoe."

Scrambling down the bank, I lost my footing and landed on my butt. Olivia caught our canoe and guided the boat into the pond then threw me the line. While I brought the canoe to shore, I started examining my pants to see if they were dirty, but all I could tell was my butt was really sore. Olivia caught the second canoe, and Everett soon joined us.

Canoeing Turtle Pond was quick with a small easy portage of a beaver dam into Slang Pond. Slang Pond was even shorter, but the portage between Slang and Long Pond required a quarter-mile hike. I got the privilege of carrying the majority of the gear, while Olivia and Everett shared in the canoe carrying. We made two trips to get all the gear and canoes to Long Pond. Once we repacked the canoes, we headed across the larger bay of Long pond, and Everett and Olivia began to search for the camp.

"You guys don't know where the camp is?" I asked.

"We're looking for a campsite to set up camp for tonight," responded Everett.

"Then why don't I see any cabins along the shore? I thought you said we would go to a great camp."

"We're going to a great campsite, not an Adirondack Great Camp. They're all privately owned, and we wouldn't be able to get into them," Everett replied.

My first impression when Everett first talked to me about this adventure was a rustic log cabin lodge with a great stone fireplace and a bearskin rug in front of the hearth, an elk antler chandelier hanging in each room, Adirondack chairs on the porch overlooking the pond with the mountains in the background. I figured the camp would have a musty smell, dust over the furniture, and mud all around the outside, but I thought I could handle it. Boy, was I mistaken! Everett and Olivia were planning on camping in tents, sleeping in sleeping bags placed on the ground, with insects flying all around them. No heat except for the fire they planned on building to cook the meals on. I don't know about you, but I really don't care for sleeping under the stars and the trees at night.

We found an empty camping spot and set the two canoes ashore. After unpacking the canoes, Everett asked me to set up my tent while he and Olivia gathered wood for a fire. I picked a spot and started sweeping the branches, stones, and even leaves with my boots, cleaning it to bare ground. Unpacking the tent was easy, but I quickly gave up on the assembly when the tent poles wouldn't go together. When Olivia returned with a handful of dead branches, she saw how frustrated I was. She took pity on me and showed me how to set the tent up. Everett came back with another armful of branches, started the fire, and set up their tent even before I was finished stowing all of my gear in my tent. I was volunteered to gather wood for the fire, and of course, I hated it because my shirt quickly became dirty from all the branches that I carried back to the fire.

Olivia cooked an excellent dinner, comparable to the finest four-star restaurant in the City. We talked for a while before sleepiness overcame me and I headed to bed. For some reason, I didn't sleep well. I kept waking every few minutes because I heard some strange noise off in the distant woods. The air mattress I slept on was comfortable, but not as comfortable as my fortieth-floor apartment bed.

I awoke to the sound of tap, tap, tap on my tent and didn't know exactly what it was until I looked out at the lake and saw the drop marks of rain. Everett and Olivia were in rain gear preparing breakfast by the time I exited my tent.

"It's raining. What a horrible day," I stated.

"That depends on your point of view," said Everett. "Days like these keep the tourists out of the woods, so there won't be as many people around to disturb the peace."

"Oh well, it looks to me like I know why the tourists don't come. They can't see anything," I said.

"So what's the plan, man?" Olivia asked in a clearly exaggerated hippie's voice.

Everett responded. "Well, we still can climb Long Pond Mountain, but we won't see anything at all with the cloud cover so low. I think we should paddle around the lake and see what else is in the area."

I asked an important safety question concerning me, "Won't the canoes sink if they get filled with water?"

"Most canoes can float even when fully submerged. It's a pain in the ass to empty them though," replied Everett.

We decided on the paddling to Rollins Pond via Floodwood Pond with a half a mile portage from Long

Pond. About a half an hour later we pushed the canoes away from camp. Because the sun was still buried behind the clouds, Everett used his map and compass to direct us to the portage. When we got there, Everett and Olivia each carried a canoe over their heads from Long Pond to Floodwood Pond, while I carried the two daypacks.

The portage was approximately a half a mile long and traversed the woods. The trail was quite wet from the continuous rainfall, which had started overnight. I passed over a small hill and noticed a portion of the trail was lined with honed logs that created small footbridges to avoid the muddy ground. With the canoes still over their heads, Everett and Olivia expertly crossed the footbridges. I stepped cautiously onto the first bridge and noticed my muddy boots were slippery on the wood, so I decided to cross it carefully by taking one step at a time. The bridge was about fifty feet long, and about halfway across it my right foot slipped ever so slightly off the wet log and landed squarely in the mud.

The mud not only covered my boot, but it rose to the middle of my calf muscle. I tried to lift my foot, but as I did, the mud resisted. I tried several more times to lift my boot out of the mud, but each time the mud just sucked my boot and foot further down. I started to panic. Should I quickly call for Everett and Olivia's help? No, they would humiliate me, and I would never live this down for the rest of my life. If I could get my boot out, I could wash off the mud in the stream at the end of the footbridge, and no one would know.

I tried one last time with all my strength, but somehow during the process my other foot slipped. I lost my balance. Loosely carrying the daypacks didn't help either as their momentum helped me fall face first into the mud. I tried to stop myself with my hands, but I could feel the slippery mud go between my fingers and jam under my fingernails. The rest of my body hit the mud with a splat, and I felt mud rain down on me. The fronts of my jacket and pants were now completely covered in mud. The two daypacks went flying a couple of yards further up the trail. I was covered in mud.

Mud filled my mouth and nose so I couldn't even scream the obscenities that were coming into my head. I tried to lift myself out of the mud, but the mud held me firm. As I lay there, I soon realized the mud was sucking me under. My body slowly sank deeper and deeper into the mud. I struggled to free myself, but continued to sink deeper and deeper into the mud. Desperately, I thrashed about using every ounce of strength that I had left, but with no better results. Breathless, I started to feel the cold mud slowly take the rest of my strength way. I knew sooner or later I wouldn't have enough strength to keep my head out of the mud as it slowly approached the surface. Then it happened, first the tip of my nose, then my nostrils. I started to gasp for every breath. If I could only call for help! I tried to calm myself with my last few breaths, thinking that this isn't the way a City person should go. Should I fight and hope that Everett or Olivia would rescue me or just sink slowly into the mud where no one will ever find my body?

As I breathed my last breath, my decision was clear. The nightmare would finally come to an end; this camping thing is not for city folk. The sweet smell and taste of fresh mud overcame my senses. My vision had turned to dark brown mud. Before I closed my eyes for the very last time, I said to myself, "This mud is not for me. The mud has won."

Slipping slowly in the mud I could hear the angels calling me to heaven.

"... En... ou..."

Peace overwhelmed me as I slipped into my grave, my body never to be seen again. Even though my body was sinking under the surface, my soul started to rise. Then an unexpected sharp pain formed across my right cheek.

"Hey, Allen, are you all right? What are you doing in the mud?" asked the familiar voice of Everett, not the heavenly voice I was expecting.

Everett slapped my other cheek, this time harder.

"What's the problem? Are you stuck in the mud or something?" he asked.

My near-death experience was over. "You've saved my life from this muddy death trap," I responded.

"You're freaking me out, man. You looked like you were having a major panic attack." Everett calmly said, "What muddy death trap are you talking about?"

"I slipped off the wood and started to sink into the mud. I almost died, but you saved my life," I answered.

"Have you looked at yourself? Your right foot is buried, and you have mud splattered on your clothes and face. How can you die from that?" replied Everett bluntly.

"I just can't explain it. You don't understand. I thought I was dying, and if you don't like that answer, then tough," I responded defensively.

"Is your boot stuck?" asked Everett. "I'll help you get it out of the mud."

"Yes, it's stuck. Can you just do it? I don't want to put my hand in the mud," I responded sheepishly after coming to my senses.

Everett ran his hand down my leg and into the mud. He scooped the mud away from my boot and soon felt the real problem.

"A branch that's attached to the corduroy is stuck in your boot lace. I'll untangle your boot lace, and you should be free," he said as he pushed my boot deeper into the mud and guided it away from the branch.

I was free of the muddy graveyard, and I placed my foot back onto the bridge.

Without another word Everett grabbed the day-packs that were lying in the mud and headed down the trail to the stream to wash the mud off his hands.

"My clothes, they're ruined!" I exclaimed.

"Why? Because you got a little mud on them?" he responded sarcastically.

"Yes," I said to my dearest of friends. "I can't handle this wilderness life; I want to go home now."

"We're not heading home. You got a taste of some Adirondack Boot-Sucking Mud, is all. My boots are caked with mud, and I'm not complaining. I love getting muddy."

We argued until we caught up with Olivia and the two canoes along Floodwood Road. She tried to convince me to stay, but I had made up my mind I wasn't camping a minute longer. Finally, they gave up and agreed if I went back to help pack up camp. I refused completely, so Everett gave me his keys and told me to walk to the parking lot and drive it back to the portage trail. As I started my walk, they grabbed one of the canoes and headed back toward Long Pond to fetch the camping gear.

No one spoke on the way home. We didn't even stop for dinner, but I had to tell someone. That's why I'm writing to you, Journal, of my misadventure and eating my General Tso's Chicken at my favorite Chinese restaurant in Midtown Manhattan…with not an ounce of mud in sight.

Chapter Three

[Searching . . .]

A 1983 two-tone brown F150 bounced down the dead-end road, flying over the potholes that the previous winter had enlarged. With a hundred thousand miles on the truck, the worn suspension was making the driver's ride more interesting with every bounce. He could feel the duct-taped seat spring poking him in his thigh every time his body was pressed into the seat from the bumps. He turned into his driveway, just missing the four-foot high boulder that held his mailbox. The truck slid to a stop in front of the porch of the converted hunting camp that he called home. Opening the driver's door, he grabbed four grocery bags from the front seat and walked to his cabin.

He walked through the living room into the small kitchen and set the groceries on the maple butcher block. He grabbed the half-gallon of milk from one of the bags just as the rotary dial phone rang. Setting the milk down, he headed back into the living room to pick up the black receiver, "Alex speaking."

On the other end of the line was his best friend, Jim Derouse. "Alex, I've finally gotten hold of you; there's a lost hiker somewhere on the Santanoni Range. The rangers need volunteers to help search, and they're gathering at the Santanoni trailhead toward Upper Works. When can you get there?"

"I need to put a few groceries away. I can be out there in about twenty minutes," Alex replied.

"Great! See you there," Jim responded, and the line went dead.

Alex replaced the receiver on the cradle and headed to the kitchen, where he grabbed the milk and placed it in the refrigerator. He checked the rest of the bags to see if any other food needed to be put away. Finding none, he hurried out to the truck and grabbed the remaining bags. Returning to the kitchen, he placed the entire bag of cold and frozen food in the freezer.

Pulling his good polo shirt off his six-foot, three-inch frame, he headed to the bedroom and threw it on the bed. The mirror above the dresser reflected his short black hair, his thin intelligent face, and his three round scars, well defined on his forty-year-old chest. He kicked off his sneakers, opened the top drawer, and pulled out a light-blue silk T-shirt and a long-sleeved fleece sweatshirt. He put both on. He replaced his denim jeans with a pair of tan nylon pants from the laundry basket. He changed to a pair of cushioned hiking socks, picked up his favorite New Hartford Whalers ball cap, and grabbed his hiking boots. With a quick pull, he lifted his full pack from beside the door onto his shoulder, held his jacket under his arm, closed the door, and headed out to his truck.

He opened the driver's door, tossed the pack onto the passenger seat, and drove down the same road that he had driven no more than three minutes before.

Twenty minutes later, Alex pulled into the parking area for the Santanoni trail. Two Department of Environmental Conservation (DEC) SUVs, a sheriff's car, a state trooper's patrol car, and two other vehicles filled most of the spaces.

Alex stepped from his truck and heard a low voice behind him ask, "When in the hell are you going to get rid of that rust bucket? I should personally give you ten vehicle and environmental citations just for driving that piece of junk here."

Alex knew the voice belonged to Deputy Sheriff Bill Outhouse, and he responded, "I'll get rid of my truck when you retire. How's that?"

"Got a piece of paper? I'll resign right now, just to piss you off and make you walk home." The sheriff broke into a wide grin as Alex turned around to shake his friend's hand. The sheriff was easily six foot, five inches and 230 pounds; his bulletproof vest made him look like one of the tree trunks that edged the lot.

Alex patted the breast pocket on his jacket and said, "Sorry, I seem to be out of paper." He laughed, turned, and followed the sheriff across the road. "So what's up?"

Rangers Doug Smith and Bill Rudd, and two others Alex didn't know, were standing around the hood of a DEC Jeep. Alex noticed that the NY state trooper was still in his patrol car.

Bill Rudd, the on-scene commander, looked over the topographical map, which was held down on the hood of his Jeep by a walkie-talkie on one end and a rock on the other. Curly white hair under the brim of his olive drab DEC Stetson hat framed his face, which was weary from doing this type of work one too many times, and much too frequently in recent years. He spoke to the men gathered around him. "The situation is this: about an hour ago 9-1-1 received a cell phone call from one David Johnson. He said that he's lost and injured, and somewhere on Santanoni. We don't know if he's on the Mountain or the Range, or if he's somewhere else. The dispatcher has tried to contact him, but he only gets his voice mail, which means that he's either out of range or has a dead battery."

"He probably can't get a signal lock on the damn thing," the deputy sheriff replied.

"Do we know what he looks like?" asked one of the rangers as he watched the low clouds moving quickly across the sky.

A dark blue Subaru Outback pulled up behind the DEC Jeep, and Jim Derouse got out and walked over to the group. Alex nodded to Jim. Rudd looked up at Jim and said, "What did you find?"

"Well, no one has signed in at Calamity Brook or the Flowed Lands since yesterday," Jim replied. He yanked off his ball cap, ran his hand through his black hair, and slapped the cap back on his head. Jim was five feet, two inches tall and was as thin as a rail, his backpack looked heavier and bigger than he did, but Jim could out-climb all of them. Jim loved being a self-made man. He was the owner of a local canoe outfitter in Long Lake, and he had all kinds of neat electronic equipment that improved the efficiency of his business.

"So is this a real call or someone just faking it?"

"I would say it's real. That silver Mercedes SUV over there checks out to be his," said the state trooper as he exited his car and walked across the road. "According to his driver's license, he's a white male, five-five, one-eighty, blond hair, blue eyes, wears corrective lenses, and is from Southhampton."

"That makes it official; we have a search and rescue on our hands," Rudd said as he looked down at the map again. "Okay, here's what we've got. Everyone knows that a man is lost and injured on the Santanoni mountain range," he said as he pointed at the map. "There is a cold front steadily moving into our area right now. The cloudbank has lowered to around 3000 feet, and it reaches to over 10,000 feet. The temperature is predicted to drop twenty degrees by morning. Currently, a little mist is falling below the cloud deck, while harder rains are predicted for later on today and into the night. Dark is in about four hours, and the helicopter is currently grounded and would be useless in helping us search until morning, when hopefully the clouds have moved out.

Bill paused to catch his breath.

"O.K., here's how this is going to work; I'm going to send three two-man teams, one for each mountain on the range. You two will search Panther," he said, pointing to the unknown rangers. "Jim and Alex, you take Couchsachraga, and Doug and I will take Santanoni. Sheriff Outhouse and Trooper Washington, you'll stay here at the command post until some more rangers arrive." The sheriff, trooper, and volunteers all nodded their assent at the assignments.

Alex spoke up, "If you want to stay here, Bill, I can search Couchie alone. Let Jim and Doug search Santanoni. I'll probably be back before everyone else will."

Bill looked Alex square in the eyes and said in a commanding voice, "I don't care if you are some highly-decorated retired Air Force PJ and have done field surgery in the middle of a battle after fast roping in, all the while wearing nothing except your boxers and boots. I don't give a care if you can carry this guy all the way down the dang mountain on your back. You know the rules. We go with a minimum of two members, and we don't split up!"

Having retired from the Air Force as an experienced 20-year veteran pararescueman, Alex had been in numerous conflicts known and unknown to the general public, saving countless American servicemen in the line of duty. Only after getting a medical discharge for injures received in a battle was he able to come home again to his beloved Adirondacks. He'd found work as an EMT in Long Lake and worked as a volunteer with the local search and rescue team. His instincts said that this search and rescue mission would be a simple walk in the park.

Alex went from a relaxed stance to attention, looking straight ahead as he responded, "Yes, sir." He awaited his orders with a smile.

The search parties gathered their packs. Alex put on his blaze orange waterproof jacket and lifted the forty-plus pound backpack onto his shoulders. Leaning forward, he latched and tightened his hip belt and shoulder straps. Alex walked to the DEC command Jeep where Bill had distributed the walkie-talkies and told them the channel they'd be using. Alex hooked his to his belt, but didn't turn it on.

"Everyone ready?" Bill asked. They all agreed, and without a word, Alex led the party into the woods.

The six men headed along an overgrown dirt road with water streaming down the tire ruts. The woods had a dark appearance and smelled of decaying vegetation. For the first half-mile of hiking, they slogged through the boot-sucking mud. Just over a mile-and-a-half in, the group turned right onto the trail headed toward Duck Hole Pond.

The trail immediately started to climb, but the seasoned searchers, with Alex in the lead, didn't even slow their pace. The nearly two-mile path and a climb of over nine hundred feet got them to the shores of Bradley Pond. Bill stopped without a word, took off his pack, and dug out his bottle of water. The other men followed suit and rested next to a fallen tree. Alex walked to the shoreline with his water filter and started to refill the nearly empty bottles.

When Alex was filling Bill's bottle, a voice from behind asked the question, "So why do you get Couchie?" Alex looked over his shoulder and saw that it was one of the rangers he didn't know. The ranger continued, "I've done it twice, I know my way over there."

Alex finished filling Bill's bottle and stood up to look at the younger ranger. "Well, first of all, I'm a four-time 46er and a two-time winter 46er. That's nearly 300 climbs around here. I grew up hiking these mountains, and I know where the official herd trail is and where most of the false ones go. I've tried them all."

Bill placed his bottle in his pack, lifted the pack onto his shoulders, turned to the young ranger, and said, "Anyway, Darrel, the hikers said that he was climbing Santanoni and not Couchsachraga. But just in case, that's where Alex and Jim are going. You might just be the hero who rescues a lost hiker."

Darrel didn't say a word; he just got ready to start the long climb to the top of the mountain range.

Bill looked at the rescue party, "Ready to move?" Bill led the men up the small herd trail.

"Hey, Bill, twenty bucks is the bet," Alex said.

"Forget it, I'm out a hundred bucks still from the last time we did this. "

"Not if it's pea soup up there. You'll probably win anyway. C'mon! We gotta make this interesting."

The rescuers climbed into the overcast clouds near 3000 feet. Initially the visibility through the fog was close to one hundred feet, but the fog soon crowded in on the search and rescue teams. Bill again reported their current position to the command post and updated them on the weather conditions.

The herd path became steeper, but the rescue party didn't slow much. Passing the sign that marked state land, the herd trail traveled westward along the contour of the mountain range. They arrived at a brook that would take them to the top of the mountain, and a flood of water was flowing down the trail. Jim said, "Hey, Alex, did you bring your fly rod with you this time?"

"No, I left it back in the truck," Alex responded.

Jim looked at the group straight-faced and said, "Looks like a good trout stream if it wasn't so damn steep."

Everyone chuckled. They continued up the brook, rock hopping and trying to keep their feet relatively dry.

"I hope this guy was smart enough to pack a few days' supply of food and warmer dry clothing. The forecast said the temperature is going to drop below freezing in the mountains tonight if this system pushes out of here fast enough," Bill said.

"How many hikers have we found lost or injured with the proper gear for the high peaks any time of the year?" Jim replied.

"Maybe one or two, but not many more," Doug said.

The increase in the popularity of hiking had brought an increase in the number of naive, inexperienced hikers who didn't know how to take care of themselves in the wild. Some simple things like rain gear, a flashlight, or even a compass could increase the chances of walking out of the woods without a problem. Recently, inexperienced hikers carried their cell phones as their only emergency equipment while hiking. They had to call for help when they got into the slightest bit of trouble, and a rescue party had to be called to find them and bring them out, just like the situation these six men faced now.

With the fog and trees getting thicker, visibility was reduced to about twenty feet. The six rescuers' outerwear was drenched, and their boots and pant legs were covered in mud. Climbing higher and higher, the trees went from maples and oaks to mountain ash, white birch, and pines. Soon the mountain ash and white birch trees disappeared. Except for the herd trail, the stunted pines grew so thick that it was all but impossible to walk through them without scratching arms, legs, and faces.

When the rescue crew reached the ridge that runs between Panther and Santanoni, they stopped for a quick rest and a progress report to the command post. The group split with Doug and Bill heading south toward Santanoni, while Alex and Jim and the two younger rangers headed north toward Panther. About halfway between the ridge junction and the summit of Panther, another trail headed west, which Alex and Jim took, leaving the two younger rangers on their mission heading north.

"Well, it looks like we're on the right trail," Alex said after he saw what looked like two fresh muddy boot prints in the muck of a mud puddle.

"Guess Bill was right to not take your bet," said Jim.

"We haven't found him yet," responded Alex.

"Why did you think he'd made his way over to Couchie, Alex?"

Alex stopped. "Well, first of all, the muddy boot impression says someone came this way not too long ago since the rain hasn't washed it away. And second, you need a line of sight for a cell phone to work in this area of the

Adirondacks. The closest cell tower is on the other side of Newcomb. That's why I think he'll be on Couchsachraga."

"Well, I hope you're right."

As they left the shoulder of Panther, they descended into a maze of dwarf pines. The herd trail between Panther and Couchsachraga can be difficult in the best of weather. With the numerous false trails, walking around the wrong side of a tree will get you lost. These false trails probably get more use than the official herd trail. With the entire mountain encased in fog, navigating the trail was difficult even for the two experienced rescue team members. After two false starts Alex found the right trail and headed across the ridge until they started to head up Couchsachraga.

When the view is unobstructed, a hiker can see the Seward range to the northwest and, on a perfectly clear day, even the Village of Tupper Lake. Santanoni is to the southeast and further east, the direction from which they had come, was Panther.

Like most of the peaks in the Adirondacks, the view from each is never the same, and you don't always get a full view. The best views can be seen from the nearby peaks in the winter when the snow pack is deep enough to make the dwarf conifers look like shrubs. With fog and rain, the two men could see only about fifteen feet in front of them.

Over the slap of branches through the stillness of fog, a voice could be heard somewhere ahead. Alex called the hiker's name. "I'm over here. Could you keep it down? I'm on the phone," replied a voice from an unseen distance.

They followed the voice until out of the flowing mist appeared the form of a man sitting on his pack with a cell phone in one hand and a PDA in the other. Jim happened to notice the man was wearing a top-of-the-line two-tone blue North Face jacket with black North Face pants that were covered with mud up to his knees.

"I've got to go. I'll talk to you later. My rescue party has just arrived," the man stated as if the two rescuers had interrupted an important business phone call in a posh downtown Manhattan office. "Hey, do you guys have any spare batteries for my GPS system? Also, before we head down, I need to recharge my cell phone. Just hiking up here drained it."

Alex asked in a commanding voice, "Sir, are you David Johnson?"

"Yeah, I'm David Johnson, " replied the man as he dug through this daypack, pulled out a small bright-yellow portable solar charger, and plugged a cable into his cell phone. He opened the charger to reveal two small solar cells and set it onto the rocks next to him. He then said, "It is going to take a long while to charge my cell phone. This fog is going to take a toll on me. Hopefully no one calls me before the battery is fully charged. I hate having to call people back."

Alex gave Jim a look of confusion. He turned to Johnson and asked, "Are you injured?"

After a few seconds of fiddling with his cell phone and charger, David responded, "Oh, are you talking to me? Sorry. What was your question?" Before Alex could reply, he added, "I'm cut up all over my arms and legs, could you look at them for me?"

Alex asked the lost hiker, "Did you hit your head at any time today?"

David shook his head as he unzipped his waterproof pant legs and slid the muddy leggings up to his knees. On the man's calves and shins were about twenty two- to three-inch red lines with small drops of incrusted blood. Jim looked at them and said, "Do you have any other actual injuries?" Looking at Jim, Alex said, "I need to check him for hypothermia if he doesn't have a concussion."

Alex removed his backpack, unzipped the front pocket, and pulled out his five-pound medical kit. Alex dug around and found the thermometer. He turned to the hiker and said, "Open up and keep it under your tongue."

The hiker did as he was told while Alex continued the medical examination. Jim took a few steps back, pulled out the walkie-talkie, and called for Bill and the other teams. "Hey, Bill, we found the hiker. So far he has just a few scratches, but Alex just started the medical exam."

"Jim, do you need any help? We'll head your way."

Jim replied, "At this time I think we can handle it, but I would say head toward the Couchie trail junction and wait there if we need you. Walking over to Couchie was pretty damn tough. We got lost a few times ourselves, and I wouldn't recommend it unless we need your help. But stay at the junction for an hour if you don't hear from us."

"We're heading back to the junction now. We'll see you there as soon," Bill responded.

Alex had finished the medical exam, and the hiker seemed to be in good condition. He was a little dehydrated, had a few scratches on his arms and legs, but there was no concussion or hypothermia.

"Hey Mr. Rescuer, are you going to treat my legs? They hurt like hell, and I feel like I'm bleeding to death," David Johnson demanded.

Alex replied, "I'll treat your legs right after I consult with my partner." And when they become gangrenous.

"Sure," Jim said, wondering what was going on, as they walked into the mist, keeping the hiker in sight.

Alex whispered, "If I didn't have to uphold an oath, I would leave this asshole out here and let him find his own way down. All he's done is bitch about his electronic crap. He doesn't even care about his own serious situation."

"We have to take him out," Jim bluntly replied.

"But this guy shouldn't be out here. He has no clue what the hell he's doing. He thinks all his gadgets will get him back to his SUV as long as he has power," ranted Alex.

"What? Didn't the Air Force give you the best and newest gadgets to help you out in your job?" asked Jim.

"But we had proper training on the equipment. And if they failed, we could always go to a simpler method. If a GPS unit failed, we just got out a map and compass. Sounds like this guy doesn't even have those!"

In the waning light the two rescuers stood in the foggy silence. The temperature was dropping.

"You want to get this guy's attention?" Jim said breaking the silence. A grin formed upon his face.

"How?"

"Just follow my lead," and he turned back toward the stranded hiker.

"Just to let you know, David, before we can treat your scratches and rescue you, we need to advise you of the fine," Jim said, keeping a straight face.

"Fine? What fine are you talking about?" David looked confused.

"Well, we're from Central Adirondack Search and Rescue, and we fine people in your situation: hikers who have no serious injuries and can get out on their own but call for help. The fine is $500, as well as the costs of this rescue," replied Jim with an authoritative voice.

"Well, what happens if I don't pay you and follow you out?" asked David.

"It doesn't really matter; DEC will impound your fancy SUV."

David sat staring at the two rescuers.

Alex started to turn, and Jim followed, disappearing into the fog and fading light.

"Wait! Wait! Wait! I'll pay," David yelled. He stood, ready to run after his rescuers, but took out his wallet and started looking through it. Pulling out his money he counted out four hundred and twenty dollars and held it out to Jim. "That's all I have."

"They'll collect the fine at the trailhead," Jim said. "Grab your pack."

"Aren't you going to carry it for me?" David asked with a pleading look on his face.

"Only if you carry mine. You didn't hire a Sherpa," Alex responded. "Leave it, I don't care."

Alex walked away so that David and Jim couldn't overhear. He pulled out the walkie-talkie, turned it on, and said, "Bill, where are you?"

After a few seconds of delay, Bill said, "About half-way between Panther and Santanoni. What's up, Alex?"

"Bill, the weather is getting bad over here. I think you should start heading down now. I'm going to bush-whack the three of us over to Duck Hole Pond using the Cold River Horse Trail. I don't know if we're going to make it out until early in the morning. We might hole up some-where, and we'll be out by noon tomorrow."

"I agree with your assessment. We'll join the party from Panther and head down. See you in the morning, and good luck," replied Bill.

Alex came back to the two men and pulled his trusted compass from his jacket pocket. Pointing toward some unseen spot, Alex said. "I have point. David, you're second and stay close to me. Jim, you bring up the rear."

Alex didn't wait for anyone. He turned and followed the compass bearing. The two men followed without saying a word. Weaving and pushing through the thick dwarf pine branches with their arms and legs, the party started to descend the very steep slope.

After the fifteenth time of getting hit with a branch in his face, arms, or legs, David spoke nervously, "I didn't come this way; are you sure this is the right direction?"

Jim yelled from the back, "Alex, can you believe a lost hiker thinks the rescue team is lost? That's just great." Ahead, Alex mentally agreed with his friend.

When the pines started to thin, Jim yelled, "Alex, you want to hold up a sec? I want to get some water."

"Sure," came a voice from below. Jim and David caught up to Alex who was holding out his bottle of water to Jim. Jim took the bottle and drank a big swig of water.

"Can I get some water?" David asked.

"What, you don't have any water?" asked Jim.

"I have water, but I was going to save it for later."

Alex opened David's pack and pulled out an unused 40-ounce commercial water bottle. He looked at the high-priced water. "Use your own water. It'll lighten your load, and we can replenish it at the base of the mountain."

David drank from his water bottle and handed it to Jim, while Alex started to descend.

Jim picked up a fist-sized rock from the ground, unzipped David's pack, and dropped it in with the bottle, quickly re-zipping the pack.

In the waning light of day, their descent became treacherous from the wet rocks and uneven footing. After David slipped for the fourth time, the rescuers stopped and waited for David to get back onto his feet. While Alex was waiting, he looked through the treetops, surveyed the ridge beyond, and said out loud, "Crap, I think we took a wrong turn. We're on the north side of Couchie; we're on the wrong path."

"What? Are you joking? I told you I didn't come this way," David yelled at the two rescuers. "I thought you guys knew where the hell you were going. You're lost; this has got to be a new one. Now the rescuer needs rescuing. Just great!"

Waiting patiently for the ranting hiker to finish, Alex finally said, "Just hold on. I said we took the wrong trail. I'm not lost. It'll take us a few more hours to hike out, but it should be easier. All we have to do is to find the Cold River Horse Trail and then head toward Duck Hole Pond."

"Fine, I'll stay while you look," David yelled at Alex.

"I don't think so. We don't leave the victim behind, no matter what," Jim replied.

Alex smiled in the darkness and said, "We could go back up to the top of the mountain. It's a shorter route."

"There's no way in hell I'm climbing back up this mountain," said David, looking up the steep slope into the darkness. With a reluctant sigh he said, "I'm exhausted."

Alex and Jim took out their headlamps from their packs and turned them on to illuminate forest before them. Jim said to David, "You better get out your headlamp."

Sheepishly David muttered, "I don't have one."

"Well, stay close to one of us so you don't trip, fall down, and break your neck. That would ruin Alex's day," replied Jim as he started to feel a little sorry for David.

They continued to descend for a while longer until the slope started to level. At that point, Alex turned the party on a northeastern heading, which would run parallel to the Cold River Horse Trail. After hiking two hours in the darkest, wettest, bushiest, coldest forest David had ever been in, they started to climb a small hill. David struggled, on the verge of collapsing from sheer exhaustion. A couple of times on this short climb, Jim yelled to Alex to hold up, but he continued at the same pace, and his headlight faded into the darkness beyond. Jim had to keep pushing David to continue. Once the men were over the hill and down the steep slope, Alex stopped next to a small pond and refilled his water bottles. Jim got his empty bottles and handed them to Alex for refilling.

David found a fallen tree, took off his pack, sat down, and said, "I don't want to complain, but I can't go any farther. I'm utterly exhausted. My feet hurt like hell."

Jim whispered, "So what do you think? Stop here or keep going? I don't think he's going to make it if we try and push him any further tonight."

Alex said, "I think you're right. We're about two miles from Duck Hole Pond and about seven back to the trailhead. The way I'm going we're cutting off about a mile, but there's still a lot of climbing and bushwhacking left. I told Bill we just might not be out until tomorrow anyway, so let's rest here tonight and get a good early start. You want to start supper? I'll start pitching the tents."

When Alex finished filling the bottle, he got his tent from his pack, found a relatively flat, dry spot, and began to set it up. Jim started his cook stove to make soup for the three of them. David sat like a bump on a log and just watched Jim and Alex work. Within half an hour supper was ready and the two tents were pitched.

When Alex finished setting up Jim's tent, Alex asked David, "So where's your tent?"

"I don't have a tent," replied David.

"You go hiking in late fall without a shelter? What would you be doing right now if we hadn't found you? You'd be sitting on Couchie, freezing your ass off, and talking on your cell phone." Alex said angrily, "Well, I guess you'll learn survival skills the hard way. You better start collecting some dry leaves to make a bed so you won't freeze to death before morning." A pause. "Well, get going."

"But, but, what about getting something to eat?" David asked with a quiver in his voice.

"What? You didn't bring extra food with you either? Well, I guess you'll also have to find some food out in the darkness, or you'll just starve. So get moving." Alex yelled like a drill instructor to a new recruit.

In the darkness, a small smile grew across Jim's face, but deep down he felt a small bit of sorrow for the man who was struggling to move off the log that he was sitting on.

"I c-c-can't move; I'm just too tired," David wanted to cry as if he were a five-year-old boy.

Alex turned toward his tent and climbed in to eat his supper as Jim stepped over and sat next to David. He said in a soothing voice, "Don't worry about Alex. Here have something to eat. You can sleep in my tent tonight."

Within a half an hour David was sound asleep in Jim's tent. Alex called from his tent, "Jim, you asleep yet?"

"No, why?"

"Is he?" Alex asked.

"Yeah." A slight pause. "You know, when I said follow my lead? I didn't mean take it over," Jim said with a hint of anger.

"Sorry. Do you think this guy will ever step inside the Blue Line again?" Alex asked.

"Don't know, but hopefully you'll teach him a few lessons anyway."

"That's all we can hope for. See you in the morning."

The night passed slowly as did the clouds, which left the Adirondacks around sunrise. With the cold, crisp, dry air, a thin fog formed, only to dissipate as the sun rose above the mountains. The tops of the highest peaks were coated in a layer of rime ice that the clouds had left behind.

The three men were abruptly awakened by a shrill electronic beeping noise. Alex dashed outside his tent.

David said from inside the tent, "Sorry, that's my cell phone. Its batteries are low. I forgot to turn it off."

Jim came out of his tent, shook his head at Alex, and said, "Nice alarm clock."

"Let's get moving since we're all up. I want to be out of here in an hour," commanded Alex.

Jim made a quick breakfast for everyone as Alex packed the tents. David hobbled barefoot out of the tent to the nearby fallen tree. "I can't walk. My feet are completely blistered." He lifted his feet to show his rescuers.

Alex stopped tearing down his tent, "Let me take a look at them."

Getting his medical kit, Alex straddled the log, lifted David's right foot, and rested it on his thigh. Alex saw the worst case of blisters he had ever seen. Blisters had formed upon blisters; some had already burst. Alex finally said, "I'm going to have to lance all of these blisters and cover them so we don't have to drag your ass out of here."

"As long as I can walk I'll be fine." David flinched when Alex touched one sore blister.

As Alex was draining the blister, he asked David, "So how many times have you been hiking anyway?"

"Yesterday was my third hike."

Alex asked as he drained another blister, "What were your first two?"

Enthusiastically David said, "Well, the first was a great hike through Central Park, and the second was about ten miles of the Long Path. Those were just beautiful days with nature."

"Let me guess. You started at Fort Lee and didn't make it outside the city limits." A nod was the response. "And you chose to hike Couchsachraga yesterday. Why?" Alex asked with a questioning look.

"A friend of mine said that I couldn't get lost with my GPS device that has a built-in map, even in the High Peaks. He said that he had trouble climbing some of the trail-less peaks, so I tried to do it myself."

"So why didn't you bring your friend along?" Jim asked, waiting for some water to boil.

"He was busy this week, but it was my day off."

Alex finished one foot then started on the other, "Couldn't you have found an easier trail to start with?"

"I thought that with all of my gadgets I wouldn't get lost hiking, even in the fog," David replied.

Alex started in on him, "Your electronic stuff, is completely worthless when it doesn't work. Without real backup equipment, like a map and compass, you're as good as dead out here."

"But what would happen if you're lost and can't find out where you are, like yesterday in the fog?" asked David.

"If you know how to use your equipment, you can navigate in the dark, like I did last night," Alex stated.

When Alex finished dressing David's blistered feet, he asked David for his socks and boots. Jim got them from the tent and handed them over to Alex. Alex looked at the pair of socks and immediately saw the answer to David's foot problems. Alex held them up and said, "You wore these socks yesterday? No wonder you got blisters that bad. These plain cotton socks give you no cushioning, no moisture control, no friction protection, no help whatsoever."

Jim stopped making breakfast, walked over to look at David's socks, and said, "You're right." He shook his head. "For as much as your winter clothing cost, your boots, your pack, and your electronic stuff, you've allowed yourself to be dependent upon a worthless pair of socks. Haven't you ever heard the story about the king's horse?" David shook his head, and Jim continued, "If the king had got a good pair of shoes for his horse, the horse wouldn't have gone lame, and the war wouldn't have been lost. You're in the same situation. You depended upon a piece of equipment that was far inferior to the rest of your equipment. I am surprised you made it that far last night." Jim turned away from David and went back to the food on the camp stove.

Alex grabbed a pair of hiking socks from his pack and gingerly placed them on David's covered feet. Alex looked inside David's boots and then knocked them together. "Gotta watch out for small creatures that like small, dark, places, for example a pair of boots. You never know when one of them is going to bite."

With that Alex let David put on his own boots. After the five-minute ordeal of tying his boots, David gingerly placed weight onto his sore feet. The pain rushed to his head, hurting every muscle and bone along the way. For a few minutes, David felt like he was being electrocuted every time he took a step, but the pain died down to where only his feet throbbed. David noticed that another place on his body hurt, and he struggled off into the woods.

Jim noticed and yelled, "Make sure you're at least a hundred yards from any body of water, and for cripes sakes don't get lost...again."

While David was out of sight, Alex went to David's daypack and emptied the contents onto the ground. He separated the rock from the cell phone, the MP3 player, the digital camera, the solar charger, and the GPS system. Alex replaced the gear and tossed the rock into the pond.

When the ripples settled, David returned from his call of nature and said, "I'm starving; when do we eat?"

Alex and Jim were already eating, and Alex said with a mouthful, "We're eating now." He paused and said, "So what did you find out there to eat for your breakfast?" He pointed toward David's call of nature route.

"Nothing. Why?" David sat on the log and scooped some food from the pot.

Alex and Jim quickly finished their meal and turned their attention back to breaking down the campsite.

David started to eat the eggs, bacon, and pancake flour concoction and said with a grin, "This is good. Can I get the recipe?"

With breakfast over and everything picked up, Alex and Jim lifted their packs and swung them around to put them on. David struggled to lift his pack. When he got it on, he said, "I don't remember this pack being so heavy."

"Oh, you're just tired," Jim said as Alex took out his compass and headed in an easterly direction.

Even in the light of the morning sun, the hiking was difficult at best, walking through scrub brush and brier patches, over boulders, and under fallen trees. They pushed through pines that were as thick as the ones near the tree lines of the high peaks as they went over a saddle point in the shoulder of Panther Mountain and then back down the other side. Soon they crossed the trail that led to Duck Hole Pond to the north and Bradley Pond to the south.

The climb to Bradley Pond was slow but steady. The two rescuers waited for the victim to climb to the top, but when he finally made it and saw the lean-to, he quickly headed for it. After taking off his pack, David sat holding his head between his knees, trying to catch his breath. He leaned back and lifted his feet. Alex and Jim started again after five minutes of rest. David hobbled to keep up with the two rescuers.

Within two hours of leaving the Bradley Pond lean-to, the two rescuers and the limping victim emerged from the trail onto the old logging road that Alex and Jim had used the previous day. Sitting on three four-wheelers were Bill Rudd, Doug Smith, and the other unknown ranger.

Bill called, as the rescue party neared, "Need a lift?"

"Yes, my feet feel like they're going to fall off any minute now," replied David. Jim and Alex just shrugged their shoulders.

The three men climbed on the backs of the four-wheelers, and they headed toward the trailhead. The tires dug through the mud and muck.

The four-wheelers struggled through the last mud holes and onto the road with the waiting ambulance. The paramedics helped David off the four-wheeler and onto the waiting gurney to be transported to the Adirondack Medical Center. Before David was loaded into the ambulance, he called out to Alex and Jim, "Thank you for rescuing me. Get me an address and I'll pay the fine. I'll even donate money every year to thank you guys for saving my life."

Jim walked over to David and said, "Don't worry about the fine right now. I'll take care of everything and send you a bill later." With a smile on his face, Jim took David's hand and shook it vigorously.

Alex came over to David, took his hand, and shook it with a vise-like handshake. He said in a quiet but firm tone, "I hope you learned your lesson. Next time I might not find you in the woods, and you'll die." Alex walked away without saying another word.

The paramedics loaded David into the ambulance and headed off to the hospital. Bill walked over to Alex and Jim and asked, "What fine was he talking about?"

Looking as innocent as children, Alex and Jim glanced at each other and responded, "Don't know."

Chapter Four

[Driving Home for Christmas]

A light green sedan was speeding north on Interstate 81, having passed through the city of Syracuse on its way to Canton. Other than having to stop for gas, food, and bathroom breaks, the occupants had been traveling seventeen hours straight from their home in the suburbs of Atlanta, Georgia. With about two hours to go, the driver yearned for the car to stop so she could start to enjoy their first Christmas together with her husband's family.

Driving all night had finally caught up with Dale. His green eyes wouldn't stay open. So around six in the morning, Susan got behind the wheel and continued the car's progress. Susan watched Dale walk around the car, and in the headlights she could see his black hair covering the top of his five-and-a-half foot slender frame. He was wearing only a light spring jacket as his southern winter coat. Underneath he wore a Thrashers sweatshirt and a pair of jeans.

Dale looked at his beautiful wife with her blue eyes, curly blond hair, the most beautiful complexion, and the cutest nose a woman could ever have. Before Dale fell asleep he said, "Stay on 81 until you get past Watertown then follow the signs to Fort Drum. Take Route 11 North until you go through Gouverneur, and then I'll tell you the way home. And if it starts to snow or there is snow on the road, wake me no matter what, and I'll drive." He knew his wife was already cold because she put on her winter leather jacket with the fur-lined hood as she moved into the driver's seat.

Susan shifted the seat back slightly so her five-foot eight-inch frame could rest comfortably while driving. She still couldn't believe Dale didn't trust her winter driving skills. She'd driven twice before in the snow, and the last time the accident that totaled her car wasn't her fault. She quietly listened to Christmas carols on the radio while she concentrated on the interstate in front of her.

Around eight o'clock the ring tone of Jingle Bells could be heard in between the seats. Susan grabbed for her cell phone and said, "Merry Christmas y'all!"

"Merry Christmas, Susan," replied her younger sister with a perfect Southern accent. "Where are you?"

"We've just passed Syracuse, and we still have a few hours to go," she said with a deep sigh. "This is one hell of a long trip. I'm going to insist that we fly next year even if we don't have the money. We have been traveling since I left work yesterday, and we're still not there."

"Better you than me. I don't think I could handle that cold weather. Have you heard the forecast for New York City? The high is going to be ten degrees tomorrow."

"Alice, we are nowhere near New York City. His parents live in northern New York, thirty miles from the Canadian border. They're an eight hour drive from New York City," Susan smartly stated in her best impression of her husband's disgusted tone of correctness.

"So, what's going on?" asked Susan, not wanting to hear the answer.

"The Weather Channel said tomorrow night is going to be twenty below. That's colder than my freezers at work. It's definitely too cold for my taste. I hope you brought your electric blanket, long johns, a parka, and mukluks."

A shiver ran down Susan's spine. Was it the result of projected cold weather, or was it just the cold in the car? Either way, she leaned over to the heater controls and turned the blower up one more notch. "Yeah, I packed plenty. Where are you?"

"In the hot tub. The kids have already opened their toys; the house is a disaster, of course."

"Sounds fun, I wish we could have been there."

"You don't sound so happy. How's Dale?"

"He hasn't spoken more than twenty words since we left. It doesn't help that one of us has been sleeping the entire trip."

"So what are you going to do?"

Susan thought for a minute and replied, "I don't know," followed by another moment of silence. "He was so much fun before our wedding, but in the last month or so he's been so depressed. I don't know what his problem is. I've tried talking to him, but he's not opening up. He's been getting worse since Thanksgiving. I just don't know what his problem is." Susan slowly shook her head.

"You could talk to a marriage..." Alice said until her thought was interrupted. "I'm back. Todd had to show me what one of his presents could do. So where was I? Oh yes, I've even read that threatening him with the big 'D' might help him wake up and smell the roses."

"Alice, I'm not going to do that. I love him."

"It's just a suggestion. Uh-oh, I've got to go. Rod and Todd are in a fight over a present. Say Merry Christmas to Dale and his family for me."

Awake, Dale said, "It's illegal to talk on a phone while driving in New York."

"Morning honey. How did you sleep?" Susan set the phone down and patted his left hand before she returned her hand back to the steering wheel.

"Not too bad. I'm stiff from sitting in the seat though. Where are we?" he asked as he shifted into a more comfortable seating position.

"We just passed the Central Square."

"Do you want me to drive?" he asked as he stretched as much as possible in the small car.

"I'm fine for now."

Waking from his dreamless sleep, Dale looked into the woods. He saw a fresh covering of snow and the bare trees flashing past. To the east the sun was traversing an azure sky broken by a handful of cumulus clouds. Directly ahead the sky was a blanket of white and growing larger as the car proceeded on its journey.

Dale had been depressed for over two months. His doctor had told him nothing was wrong physically or mentally and had prescribed him anti-depressants. He didn't want to take the medication until he understood the why, but he knew the depression was affecting his marriage. Susan's family tried to help, but so far nothing had worked. Susan suggested a trip to his parents' home might help since they haven't seen them in nearly a year. With every passing mile a mental weight started to lift from Dale's mind, and a small thin smile formed across his unshaven face.

The dry smooth highway went from last year's blacktop job to old broken concrete. The tires thudded over all the gaps while the two of them were jostled relentlessly.

Susan stated without expecting an answer, "This pavement is rough."

"It's because there isn't enough ice on the road yet for the State to bring out the 'Zambonis.'"

Susan chuckled and a small smile formed across her face as she realized her husband had made his first smart-ass remark in months.

A moment later the sun disappeared as the car drove under the white blanket of clouds. Flakes of fluffy white snow started to blow across the highway. Seeing the snow, Dale became fully awake and noticed that fresh snow was starting to build on the edges of the dry pavement. He said, "Susan, pull over and let me drive."

"Why? I've driven in snow before."

"Not what's in front of us, you haven't. Pull over now before we can't see where the hell we're going and slide off the road," Dale responded with a hint of excitement.

With his fatherly guidance Susan slowly pulled onto the shoulder of the highway. Dale opened his door and walked around the front of the car, while Susan slid to the passenger's seat. Dale tried to open the driver's door, but it was locked still. He waited until Susan opened it up. Susan shivered as the cold air hit her face. Dale adjusted the seat and mirrors, shifted the car into drive, and pulled back onto the highway.

Within a few miles a light snow started to fall. The two-mile visibility dropped to a mile. The snow piled onto the shoulders and slowly covered the passing lane. The other drivers reduced their speed to the actual speed limit, driving more cautiously and testing the road conditions.

Passing the exit sign for Tinker Tavern Road, they were engulfed in a white cloud of snow. The visibility dropped to less than a quarter mile. The darkened highway was covered in two to four inches of snow. All the vehicles traveling in this section of Interstate 81 slowed to a crawl and formed one continuous line of traffic. Each driver now depended on the driver in front of him. Everyone was searching to know where the road was.

After riding for a few more minutes in silent disbelief, Susan said, "Is this what you would call a whiteout?"

Dale, concentrating on the fifty feet of road and taillights in front of them, slowly answered, "Yep, this is what I'd call a lake effect whiteout. I've seen worse up here though including zero visibility."

"Last year the weathermen said Atlanta had whiteout conditions, but this is nothing like what I saw."

"That's because most weather forecasters have no clue what a whiteout really is. That includes the winter weather specialist from the Weather Channel."

"How fast are we going?"

"Twenty-one."

"Is this a bad time to tell you that I have to pee?"

"Yeah, since I'm not pulling over until we get through the lake effect."

"How long will that take?"

"You got me. We could drive out of it in a few miles, or we could be driving through it well past Watertown."

With everything completely white except for the dimly lit taillights in front of them, time slowed down for Susan. She watched individual snowflakes tumble toward the road. A few flakes caught the car's slipstream, passed slowly over the hood and then the windshield. Other snowflakes failed to make the trip, falling apart on the windshield, where they either melted very quickly or were swept away by the windshield wipers. Every few seconds the wipers cleared the watery snow from the windshield, sweeping the slush into an ever-building pile. Eventually the windshield wipers were covered with snowy ice, and so was the windshield itself. Snow already covered the other windows, making them useless. For several seconds Susan lost the taillights in a blanket of crystal white. Her eyes searched frantically for the taillights. A scream of sheer panic formed at the back of her throat. The taillights then reappeared. Her heart skipped a beat as she let out a sigh of relief to calm herself.

Dale's attention was completely focused on the task of driving. The smile had become a grin because these driving conditions were easier than his daily drive in six lanes of bumper-to-bumper traffic. He hated every minute of his daily commute, especially when it rained and then traffic accidents jammed the highways. Dale knew he could outdrive any Southerner on any wintery road in the South. Anyone who's lived in northern New York for any length of time learns how to handle a car on slick roads, as well as following the tracks of the driver in front of you when you can't see where you're going.

An SUV with North Carolina tags flew past the car.

"Why don't you follow him?" asked Susan.

"I don't want to follow him into the ditch, that's why," replied Dale bluntly.

"Oh." A pause. "I think I can disprove the theory."

Dale took a glance at his wife and said, "What?"

"If it snows this much in one storm, the probability is one that two snowflakes will be alike somewhere in this one storm. You just have to find them."

Dale chuckled and, with a growing smile, said, "Be my guest."

Progress through the snow was slow, making that last few miles take forever. The taillights periodically disappeared. Even the traffic slowed as the snow fell harder. Traveling at a snail's pace, Susan noticed an SUV in the ditch through her snow-covered window. The driver was attempting to get traction but was just spinning his wheels.

"Dale, there's an SUV in the snow bank. Should we stop to help him?"

"No, he's the idiot that passed us a few minutes ago."

"Should we call for a tow truck?"

"You can call 9-1-1 to notify the state troopers, but he's stuck. They won't be getting him out until the snow stops and the roads are plowed. Anyway, he probably has a cell phone and has already called."

"I thought that you said northern New Yorkers were always helpful in a time of crisis."

"We are extremely helpful to our friends and neighbors. He's the idiot that drove too fast."

The subject was quickly dropped when the taillights in front of them disappeared, this time for over two solid minutes.

Holding her breath, Susan started to pray for taillights to return.

Slowing down, Dale followed the barely visible tracks ahead, feeling the car's performance for a change when he meandered out of the track and made the careful and appropriate correction.

Mesmerized at the unchanged scenery, Susan thought only ten minutes had gone by, but in reality a full hour had elapsed. When Susan's cell phone rang, she snapped back into reality, picked it up, and said, "Hello?" She sat, lost in thought, and finally in a trembling tone said, "Merry Christmas."

"Susan, you all right? Where are you?" Buck, Dale's father, was on the other end.

"I'm fine, just a little scared," she responded. "It's your father," she said to Dale. "He wants to know where we are," she told Dale in a calmer voice.

She then returned to the call, "I think we just passed Pulaski. Why?"

"Shit, you're already in it. Damn." Dale clearly overheard his father.

"Wh... Wh... What's wrong?" Susan asked fearfully.

"Channel Seven is announcing that 81 North and Southbound closed from Coffeen Street to Central Square because of the lake effect blizzard. Watertown is getting six to eight inches an hour."

Susan relayed the news to Dale.

"They announced a State of Emergency for Lewis, Jefferson, and Oswego Counties with no unnecessary road travel. All roads are closed to through traffic."

"Nice time to tell us, considering we're already in the middle of it," responded Dale.

Trying to absorb all this new information, Susan asked, "What is a lake effect blizzard?"

"Its an upgraded lake effect winter storm that has blizzard conditions with falling snow, extremely reduced visibility, and gusting winds of over thirty-five miles per hour," replied Buck.

Susan could not fully comprehend their situation.

"Mom said another news update just came on." Buck paused to get the new information. "Oh, my God!" A long pause. "Watertown is pulling their plows off the road until the storm is over. I have never heard of anything like that." Buck's worried voice was coming through the phone as thick as the snow that was already covering the car's windshield. "How are the roads?"

"Bad. I can barely see the car ahead," replied Susan.

"Tell Dale to drive safely and if you get stuck, call us immediately. Uncle Dave and I will come get you. Stay warm, and we'll see you when you get here."

Susan turned the phone off.

Buck sounded worried, and that made Susan more nervous. She was even getting to the point of feeling sick to her stomach. She tried to hide her emotions, but Dale saw that she was starting to turn as white as the snow outside.

"Can you find me my sunglasses?" Dale asked.

"Why do you want your sunglasses?"

"Hopefully they'll cut some of the glare down, and I'll be able to see the tracks better," Dale explained.

Susan searched most of the car and finally found the sunglasses in the glove box. She handed them to Dale.

The slow caravan of vehicles was progressing north, passing unlucky motorists who were stuck in the snow banks on the side of the road. As the same scene repeated itself every mile, Susan started to relax. She was becoming more confident in Dale's driving abilities.

Concentrating on driving, Dale knew he shouldn't be smiling about their predicament, but he was and couldn't help himself. He was happy to see this snow surrounding him. The falling snow reminded Dale of all the sledding on the hill behind his parent's house that he, his older brothers, and cousins did every day growing up when snow fell. He recalled the cross country ski trips with his mother through the back country of the High Peaks, the school sponsored trips to snowboard on Whiteface and Gore. He could almost feel the cold wind in his face from snowmobiling on the hundreds of miles of backcountry trails throughout the Adirondacks. Those were the best days, Dale thought to himself.

After driving two hours in the snowstorm, the windshield wipers were almost covered in ice. A large section of the windshield wasn't being cleared. Dale didn't want to stop and scrape the windshield, so he did the next best thing. Rolling down his window, he stuck his hand outside and grabbed the moving wiper to knock the ice off the blade.

Susan was shocked to see him open the window with the snow blowing everywhere. She was flabbergasted to watch her husband climb halfway out of the car to grab for the wiper blade.

"Are you nuts?" Susan screamed. "Climbing out of a moving car to clean the windshield? Why didn't you pull over and do that? I'm covered in snow! I'm freezing." She brushed some of the snowflakes off her coat. Underneath she was shivering.

"I didn't want to get stuck in the snow if I pulled over," replied Dale.

An hour later they passed under the Coffeen Street Bridge, and the falling snow just disappeared. The roads were still slushy, but improved to the point where traffic accelerated to half the posted speed limit. Upon seeing the world again, Susan took a deep breath and slowly released it. She calmed her nerves and tried to stop shivering.

Exhausted, Dale looked over to her and said, "Now that's a lake effect blizzard."

"Can we stop somewhere so that I can pee? I really have to go," Susan pleaded.

"We take the next exit. There's a Mickey D's a few miles away on Route 11."

"Fine. I can hold it that long."

Looking at the surrounding countryside, Susan saw a Christmas dream come true that she would never see at home. The white puffy clouds disappeared, and crystal clear blue sky emerged. With the lake effect storm drifting south, the fields were covered in fresh hip-deep powder snow. Every branch from the smallest twig to the thickest limb was covered with snow, making the woods look like they floated in the clouds. All the cars traveling northbound were covered in over six inches of snow. Snow blowing off the cars created small whiteouts behind them then the cars' true colors were finally revealed.

They pulled into the Mickey D's parking lot where Susan hurried into the fast food joint looking for relief. Dale got two coffees to go as he waited for Susan to finish in the bathroom. Heading back to the car, Susan took the coffee while Dale grabbed the snowbrush to clean the snow off the car.

Susan set the coffee in the car but stood in the ankle deep snow of the parking lot, watching her husband work barehanded as he brushed the snow off of the car. Snow started to melt down the inside of her boots, wetting her socks. A white mist formed with every breath she took. With each exhale a little more of her anxiety melted away in the frigid air. Standing in this winter wonderland, a faint smile fell across her face. She became very present in the moment and amazed that she had survived the most terrifying ordeal of her life, a lake effect blizzard.

"Dale, were you scared driving through that?"

"I wasn't scared. I was too busy driving to be scared," replied Dale.

"After your father hung up, I was scared to death. I've never been that scared in my life. I thought we'd be in a massive pileup, both of us frozen to death, and our bodies wouldn't be found until Spring. But now that we're through the storm..." Susan bent over, scooped up a fistful of snow in her gloved hands, made a snowball, and threw it at Dale.

The snowball broke up in flight as it sailed past Dale's head. Dale stopped brushing the car, grabbed a large handful of snow barehanded and compressed it as tightly as possible. "That was a pathetic attempt of a snowball."

Dale threw his at Susan, hitting her squarely in the chest. The snowball made a thump and left some remnants on her jacket as it crumbled upon impact. An ear-to-ear grin formed on Dale's face.

Susan noticed this and said, "This is the first time I have seen you smile in two months." Susan grabbed more snow from the top of the car and threw it at her husband. "What's changed? It's not that you're near home, is it?"

"No, I think it's the snow. I didn't start feeling better until we started driving into the lake effect. Now I think the fresh snow has invigorated me, restored me, lifted the weight off me, and released my Christmas spirit. I would never have considered that I missed the snow this much, but I do. It is something that brings back fond childhood memories. It all takes me back to when I was carefree and everything appeared to be peaceful no matter what else was happening in the world. The fresh fallen snow makes the world seem like a clean and beautiful place to enjoy with everyone including my beautiful, caring wife."

A snowball hit Dale in the side of the face, and he retaliated with a quick barrage.

The customers inside the warm fast food joint watched the two having a ten-minute snowball fight. Wet and covered in snow, they embraced and kissed for just as long as they had fought in the snow. Then they left the parking lot on their way to a merry Christmas.

Chapter Five

[The Catch of the Day]

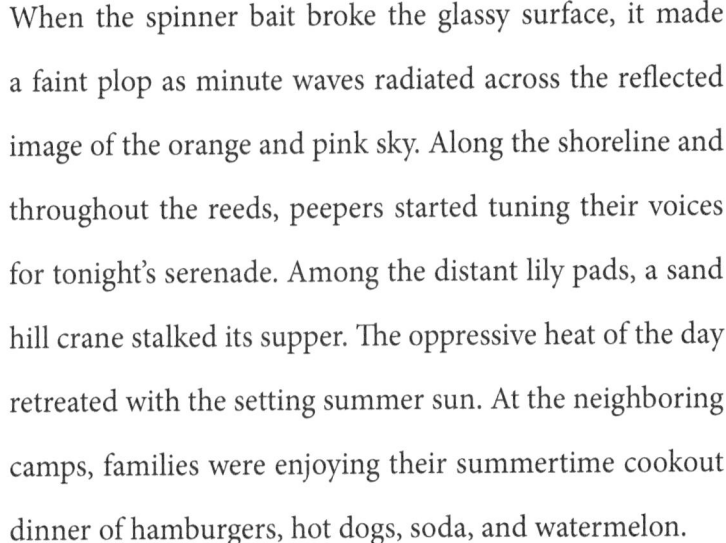

When the spinner bait broke the glassy surface, it made a faint plop as minute waves radiated across the reflected image of the orange and pink sky. Along the shoreline and throughout the reeds, peepers started tuning their voices for tonight's serenade. Among the distant lily pads, a sand hill crane stalked its supper. The oppressive heat of the day retreated with the setting summer sun. At the neighboring camps, families were enjoying their summertime cookout dinner of hamburgers, hot dogs, soda, and watermelon.

With only his swim trunks on, Noah, a blond-haired teenager stood on a rickety dock that jutted out into the water some twenty feet. He retrieved the spinner bait with his trusty fishing pole. Having lived for the past fifteen summers at the camp, he knew the rickety dock wouldn't collapse. Even if it did manage to give in this year, the short swim back to shore would be refreshing, not dangerous. After supper Noah always enjoyed going for a quick dip because he worked long hard days mowing lawns for the local landscaper.

Across the lake a small bass boat steered past the channel marker and on around Scout Island on the Great Sacandaga Lake. It slowly approached the camp. Noah knew his father, Dennis, was at the helm of the boat while Mark, his older brother, was at the stern, trolling. Noah knew it must be close to suppertime if these two die-hards were returning from a day of fishing on the lake. He also knew that after supper the three of them would head out again for some nighttime fishing. For the men in his family, fishing wasn't just a sport or a hobby. It was an obsession.

Noah continued casting the spinner bait and was slowly retrieving it. He anticipated a strike at any second.

With his new summer job he couldn't devote the time to fishing he once had, and that's why he was fishing from the falling down dock now.

The boat pulled alongside the new dock his family had built last year. Noah waved to his father and brother as they lashed the boat to the dock's cleats. Leaving everything in the boat except the trash and a cooler, the two men walked over to the old dock to greet the youngest member of their family.

"Catch anything?" Dennis asked, his deeply tanned face barely showing under his large-brimmed straw hat.

"Not yet. You?" replied Noah, with a slight hint of disappointment in his voice.

His father responded with his usual quiet relaxed attitude, "Not a bite all day."

"Not a good day for fishing, that's for sure," Mark replied. His face was just as tan, but he wore his own kind of a lucky fishing hat. "I think all the school fish are on summer vacation," he quipped.

They chuckled, even though it'd been said before.

"Well let's go and get washed up for supper. Your mother wants me to get the grill ready."

"I'll be along shortly, I want to cast a few more times," Noah said.

"Fine," responded Dennis as the two men turned and headed toward the forty-year-old camp.

Casting again, Noah let the spinner bait sink a few seconds longer than normal before he started to reel it back slowly. After hearing the dismal fishing report, Noah's anticipation subsided. His enthusiasm about catching a fish slipped from his mind. Lately, he'd been thinking hard about his whole future, not only the rest of this summer, but college life and beyond. The one thing that calmed his anxious thoughts was fishing.

Suddenly the reel became hard to crank. The line became taut. His rod tip bent towards the water. Waking up from his daydream, Noah pulled back on the rod, setting the hook. The rod bent even more, forming a skewed question mark from the side. He yelled, "Hey, I got something."

Realizing the line hadn't moved, Noah muttered to himself, "Damn it, I've hooked a log."

He pulled back hard on the rod, hoping the line wouldn't break because he didn't want to search for the spinner after supper. But the line didn't break or move.

Dennis and Mark returned to the dock, and then his father asked, "What do you have?"

"Ah, I think I'm hooked on something," Noah said with frustration.

Lowering the rod tip eased the tension on the line, and Noah reeled in the slack line. Having hooked logs, rocks, and weeds hundreds of times, Noah moved the rod from side to side, trying to free the hook and spinner bait. Not getting the desired result, Noah clamped the line next to the rod with his hand, removing the tension from the reel. He pulled on the line, trying to break it if necessary.

The line moved.

Noah reeled in the slackening line.

Dennis stared at the point where the line and water met and noticed it continued to move after the line went slack. In amazement he responded, "What in the hell do you have on the end of that line?"

He barked to Mark, "Get the net!"

Mark ran to the boat and retrieved the two-foot wide landing net.

"You don't think I have a log, do you?" Noah asked.

"Nope," replied his father, who had all the confidence in his son's ability to land whatever was on the other end of the line. "What pound test line do you have?"

"I'm using four-pound test," responded Noah, who didn't give the question another thought as he concentrated on bring the prize home. "Either I've got a turtle or one hell of a fish. If it's a fish, he's not running like any other fish I've ever hooked before."

"Don't lose it. I want to find out what it is," Mark said, slightly out of breath as he returned with the net.

"If the line snaps, I'm going after it," replied Noah.

Simultaneously Dennis and Mark said, "I'll be right behind you."

Noah pulled and reeled like a deep-sea fisherman. The work was tediously hard as the line slowly approached the dock. The minutes passed, and all three men prayed that neither the pole nor the line would snap at the last second. Once the line was close to the dock, Noah gently raised the rod, which bent into a full arch, lifting more of the line out of the water. Mark dipped the net and scooped directly up under the line. As they lifted the fishing net with the catch, the tension released on the fishing pole, which straightened to its normal shape. Mark set the net and its contents on the dock. All three men examined the catch realizing that it wasn't a log, a turtle, or even a record-sized fish.

Minutes passed while the three stared at the net in disbelief. The net contained six silt-covered cans of beer connected by a six-pack ring with the spinner bait hooked to one of the can lips.

Dennis responded first, "Noah, you're not old enough to catch that type of fish; you'll have to throw them all back." A grin formed across his face.

Trying to suppress his laugher, Mark asked, "How in the hell did a six pack end up on the bottom of the lake?"

"We definitely need to take a picture of this catch," Dennis said, as he started to chuckle.

"Luckily, I've got a camera with me." Noah pulled a digital camera out of his pocket and handed it to his father.

Noah grabbed the six-pack and held it like a trophy fish as his father took the picture.

"I wonder if Mom would like to make beer batter beer can for supper," Mark said with a straight face.

"It would taste good, but it might be a little too hard to swallow," replied their father.

From the camp's porch Noah's mother yelled down, "Dennis, Mark, Noah! You coming up for supper or not?"

"Let's get going," Dennis said. "Bring your catch or your mother won't believe us."

The three men headed toward the camp.

"I think I'm going to have sushi tonight," Dennis stated to his sons.

"Where are you going to get sushi? All Mom has is hamburgers and hot dogs to grill since you didn't catch any fish today," replied Noah.

"And this one's going to college," Dennis said as he pointed his thumb at Noah while he looked at Mark. He grabbed a beer can, popped its top, and took a long swig. "Ah, the best sushi ever, right temperature and everything!"

After a moment Noah finally began to laugh with his father and brother. Noah knew today would be with him forever, no matter where his future life might take him, because today he had the best catch of the day.

Chapter Six

[Breakdown]

"Just great! This ruins a perfectly good weekend," Killian Wethomer yelled to himself. He threw his hands against the steering wheel in frustration as his manual sport utility vehicle coasted along. Killian attempted to downshift and steered the vehicle onto the wide shoulder of the road before it stopped completely. Giving one last try, he floored the pedal and popped the clutch. The screaming engine redlined, which was deafening in the cabin interior. When he removed his foot from the gas pedal, the engine died with a clunk-clunk sound. The 2002 rover finally had stopped for good. Without even trying to restart the engine, he screamed, "Damn it!"

Exiting the SUV, Killian slammed the door, almost breaking the window's tempered glass.

Killian's baby-faced head barely cleared the roof rails of the large SUV. A green "Free The Planet" t-shirt and a pair of knee-length, gray cotton shorts covered his thinly built, bronze body. Dirt and brown leather sandals covered his feet. His shaggy, dirty-blonde hair was matted in places from wearing a Rensselaer Polytechnic Institute ball cap and wild in other places where he ran his hand through his sweat-covered hair. Being twenty and carefree was fun, but missing the review session for his Calculus final at RPI was frightening because he needed all the help he could get to pass the test and the course.

On the deserted two-lane road Killian stomped and yelled around the rover as he inspected the vehicle. He didn't find anything noticeably wrong with the vehicle, but this didn't surprise Killian since his knowledge about cars was minimal. He knew to fill the gas tank when the needle approached "E," but this needle wasn't on "E" yet.

Today, a few miles back, a terrible mechanical grinding noise started. A vehicle like this shouldn't make grinding noises, and Killian didn't want to be stranded in the middle of nowhere. His fear only intensified his ill-fated decision to press on down the road to get as far as he possibly could. However, Murphy's law prevailed. With a big bang, the service engine lights switched on and the rover started to coast.

Killian considered that someone would eventually come and help him. New York State Route 30 was always heavily traveled compared to the rest of the Adirondack Park. Killian scanned the road about a half a mile in each direction. Seeing no trace of human activity except for the road, a couple of telephone poles, and a whole mess of litter, he knew it would be a long wait. After calming down, he climbed back into the SUV, where he searched unsuccessfully for a cell phone, a map, or anything that would help him get back to civilization and his dorm room in time for the review session.

Finding nothing, he fumbled around the steering column until he turned on the hazard lights. He rolled down the windows to let the cool summer breeze blow through the rover. He inserted his favorite CD into the stereo and cranked up the volume. Putting his head back with his eyes closed, he relaxed and listened to the heavy metal music flowing through him. He thought with irritation, "I can't believe my luck. Everything was perfect for this weekend: the weather, the hiking partner, the views, and even the meals. I can't believe this perfect weekend is going to cost me my entire college career."

A car flew by.

When Killian opened his eyes and saw the car wasn't slowing down, he shook his head and thought, "Tourists. Always in a rush. No time to help someone in need along the side of the road. Hmm."

Enveloped in the music, Killian closed his eyes again and listened for what seemed like hours. He opened his eyes and saw a sheriff's patrol car with its lights flashing in the rearview mirror.

His heart stopped. Sheer panic set in. A sinking feeling grew and grew in the pit of his stomach. He felt queasy. He stopped breathing.

Seconds seemed like minutes, and minutes seemed like hours.

An eternity of seconds seemed to pass when Killian realized the sheriff had stopped to help him. He inhaled deeply to calm himself. He tapped several buttons on the stereo, and the CD ejected. The rover became silent enough to hear his pounding heart trying to escape from his chest.

The deputy sheriff emerged from the car, carefully walked to the front driver's side door, and said through the open window, "Excuse me, sir. Do you need assistance?"

Having been pulled over before for three speeding tickets, Killian came out of his stupor and said, "Th-th-this rover just died. It made some noises and a bang. I don't know what happened."

"How long have you been here?"

"Oh, I would say about fifteen, twenty minutes."

"Have you called for a tow truck yet? It's a long way to Speculator, even longer to Indian Lake."

"I don't have a cell phone. If you could call one for me, I would appreciate it," Killian replied as he looked into the deputy's face with an ear-to-ear grin of joy.

"Where are you headed?"

"RPI. I'm taking a summer class, and my final is in the morning," Killian responded. He started to feel his stomach tighten as the deputy continued to ask questions.

"Where were you coming from?"

"I hiked Pillsbury Mountain and camped around Pillsbury Lake this weekend."

"Nice weekend to get out. I wish I had more time to take off and do some backpacking." Tapping the SUV with his hand, the sheriff said, "Must have run into thorn apple or a briar patch; you got drops of blood behind your ear."

Feeling the crusted drops with his fingers, Killian said, "Yeah, I didn't see it until I was already in it." A pause. "I've got scratches all over my body."

"Okay, hold on tight, and I'll get you on your way so you don't miss your final. I'll call for a tow truck. It shouldn't be more than an hour for Jeb to show up." The deputy headed back to his car.

Killian breathed a sigh of relief. He always felt nervous around any law enforcement officers, even though deep down he knew an officer could be trusted to serve and protect.

Both men waited patiently in their vehicles for the tow truck as the daylight faded fast. The flashing lights from the patrol car started to cast shadows of Killian's head on the interior of the rover. Sitting nervously, he wanted the tow truck to arrive so the sheriff could leave. Taking a glance back between the bright flashing lights, he saw the deputy was sitting in his car doing paperwork. Just at that moment the deputy looked up at him. He turned back around in the driver's seat and closed his eyes. He let his thoughts run. Leave! Please, leave! When is the tow truck coming? I've got a final to take in the morning. Even if I leave now, I won't get back until midnight. Maybe the deputy can give me a note or something for my professor. When will that tow truck show up? I want the sheriff to leave.

Killian hit the rover's horn with his fist as hard as he could to blow off some steam. The horn sounded louder than he expected as it echoed off the nearby trees in the deserted area.

Awakened from his angry rage, Killian tried to calm down when he remembered the sheriff's patrol was still behind him. The rearview mirror showed the deputy wasn't in his car. But the driver's side mirror revealed the shadowy figure of the sheriff approaching the SUV. Killian said to himself, "Calm down. Calm down. Everything will be all right. I just have to wait until the tow truck comes." Just think of the perfect little weekend we had.

"Sir, is everything all right?" The sheriff stood a step away from the driver's door, while shining his flashlight into the vehicle.

Killian placed his hands on the steering wheel and said with a smile, "Everything's fine, Officer. I bumped the horn when I was looking for a piece of candy on the floor. It fell down by my feet." A pause. When is he going to leave? "Is that all?" Killian asked as the sheriff turned toward his car. "Thanks for asking," he said, and after a moment, "How much longer until the tow truck arrives?"

The sheriff returned to the window. "Don't know, a serious accident occurred about twenty minutes ago near North Creek, it sounds like a moose was involved. It could be a couple more hours. You sure you're all right? I could drive you to North Creek and drop you off at Jeb's Garage. You could wait there and call someone to come get you."

"I'm okay, I'll wait. Thanks anyways." Killian slumped back into the seat. He was starting to feel more desperate and depressed about his situation.

As the sheriff returned to his patrol car, he shined the flashlight into the back of the rover and saw Killian's full-pack sticking above the seats. Returning to his patrol car, the sheriff went back to his overdue paperwork.

Killian thought to himself, I can't believe this cop isn't going to the accident. There might be a seriously injured person who needs his help. He could even help save one of the sacred moose of the Adirondacks. All I need to do is drop off this piece of shit and make my way back to my dorm. Killian knew he needed to take control of his emotional state before it got him into serious trouble. Remembering his perfect camping weekend would help him relax and allow him to regain a calmer emotional state.

[~]

Two men finally entered a small clearing on top of Pillsbury Mountain after hiking for hours on a continuously climbing trail. The fire tower loomed over them as the observer's cabin sat quietly next to the steel tower. The blue sky and warm sun were perfect with the gentle breeze blowing on top of the mountain, which cleared out the gnats and flies.

Killian walked over to the porch of the observer's cabin, removed his heavy backpack and sat down. Even though he wasn't really that tired, he wanted a moment to reflect on his trials and tribulations while climbing up the mountain. He always enjoyed coming to the mountain to reinvigorate and recharge his mental capacity. The lack of people, light and sound pollution, and commercialism always helped his mood. Up here, away from the cities, towns, and villages, someone can lie on the ground and completely enjoy nature in its proper setting.

"Hey, are you going to climb to the top?" asked Gill.

Killian quietly replied, "Maybe."

Gill, a well-dressed hiker with expensive clothing and gear, quickly dropped his pack and climbed to the top of the fire tower. His dark businessman's haircut reflected the sun enough to make his head shine white. His well-groomed and athletic physique made easy work of this moderately difficult climb. Even his chiseled face was properly shaved this morning with only the start of a five o'clock shadow showing.

"Wow, what a view! I never believed you could get such an awesome view from a fire tower. Hell, I climbed Mount Rainier last year and I thought that was excellent, but this one ranks right up there. Oh, there's Snowy and Sacandaga." As Gill spun around looking at everything, he said, "Wow, look at those lakes, they look like perfect places to go trout fishing. Hey, have you gone trout fishing before?" A pause. "Well, I went to Montana a few years back and was guided down the Yellowstone River. I caught a 25-pound rainbow trout, the most beautiful fish I've ever seen in my life. It took me an hour to land him. It's mounted over my office desk. Hey Killian, do you like fishing?"

Can he just shut up for a minute? Thought Killian while he replied, "Yes."

"Great! I know a great recipe we can try tonight if we catch a couple of trout. You'll die and think you've gone to heaven. A guide in Alaska taught me. Hey, why don't you come up here and see the sights, the view sucks from down there. You can't even see beyond the first set of pine trees."

Killian made his way slowly up the steps, stopping one flight below Gill. He tried to soak in the sun as well as the peacefulness of the surrounding Adirondacks. But his peace was cut short when Gill started to talk about his last court case and how he got the defendant, an ATV club, off of a trespassing charge when some of their ATVs crossed private property to get access to a public trail.

I want quiet, you idiot. Can't I stand here and just admire the views without listening to your talking? Killian made his way down the stairs and back over to his pack where he got out a bottle of water and took a few sips. He was slightly disappointed in the view.

After ten minutes of continual talking from the top of the fire tower, Gill finally headed down. Retrieving his pack, Gill finally asked Killian, "You ready to head down?"

With a deep sigh, Killian replied, "Yep."

[~]

My perfect weekend, I've been planning it forever. Visiting the hiking and outdoor chat rooms, meeting and e-mailing people whom I've never met. I don't know why I'm shy. But for some reason the Internet allows me to open up and access the world. When I'm online, no one knows how shy I really am. For most of my life I've been lonely, but not anymore, the World Wide Web is my best companion. I have met all of my best friends on the 'net. I don't care that I don't know their real names, all I care is that there are more people like me, a shy college kid trying to live in this information overloaded society. A screen name is just a persona. Just this morning I found out that ATVLawyer01 is Gill.

Gill, huh... Gill just couldn't shut his big trap. He's the reason my perfect weekend is ruined!

Killian grunted angrily. He looked back in the flashing mirror and said with a menacing voice, "When are you going to leave?"

Calm down, calm down. You don't want the sheriff asking any more questions, do you? Just calm down and relax. Think about how you fixed the problem to keep your weekend perfect even though you'd never met a person before who didn't stop talking for more than two seconds, not even to catch their breath.

[~]

After making the hike down Pillsbury Mountain and retrieving Gill's external backpack from his vehicle, Gill and Killian hiked their way to the shores of Pillsbury Lake. After traversing around the north side of the lake, they set their campsite up in a relatively level spot near the shore of the quiet and serene lake.

"I think this would make the perfect spot," stated Gill as he looked toward the lake and saw Pillsbury Mountain in the background. "When the sun comes up, it will rise over the mountain tomorrow morning and will make a beautiful picture. Let's start setting my tent up and getting the food going. How would you like steamed lobsters?"

Killian looked at him with a quizzical look.

"I'm joking. I've got Katmandu curry and hot apple cobbler for dessert. I've never had freeze-dried meals, so hopefully they will compare with the four-star dining that I am used to eating during the week."

Killian dropped his pack and unpacked his tent.

"You might want to consider getting a ground-cloth before you go camping again. That way your tent will last longer," Gill stated, sounding like one of Killian's professors grading his work. "You know," a momentary pause. "From what I've seen today I think the ATVer that sued the State for more access to the trail will love this place. I'll have to tell him about it when I file our new lawsuit."

Night could not come soon enough for Killian. As Gill prepared for sleeping, Killian walked to the shoreline and sat quietly on a pile of rocks. When Gill finally fell asleep, the quiet emanated throughout the woods. Killian watched the moon rise above Pillsbury Mountain, creating a perfect reflection off the mirror-like lake surface. In the distance a screech owl called. Killian thought he'd never seen so many stars in his life. For the first time since meeting Gill, Killian was at peace with his environment.

I absolutely love the peace and quiet this wilderness provides me. Hiking alone in the wilderness can produce such insight into one's soul. It allows time to contemplate life and how I can change the world. But every time I go back to the real world I break the promises I've made to the plants and animals. My commitment tonight is to improve my planet, because I'm the only person who can.

The last minute e-mail to Gill worked perfectly, convincing him that we should hike Pillsbury Mountain and camp on the shores of Pillsbury Mountain instead of the Northville-Placid Trail. I loved my line, "The N-P Trail will be overcrowded this weekend. Let's hike someplace more remote with more beautiful vistas." I'm surprised he immediately replied, agreeing to the change.

The loudest, most disturbing noise that Killian had ever heard roused him from his peaceful, nighttime reflection. Reverberating through the darkness, the noise was so horrendous that Killian knew of no creature great or small that could make it, except one.

Gill's snoring sent shivers through Killian's body worse than any set of fingernails scraping a chalkboard could ever create. All the animals in earshot are running to find the nearest pool of water to drown themselves, just to save themselves from the misery.

[~]

Emerging from his trance, Killian noticed a half an hour had passed, and the deputy was still behind him. He muttered to himself, "It must be a slow night." After a momentary pause he banged the steering wheel and said, "When is that tow truck getting here?"

The combination of sitting still, hiking all weekend, being frustrated about the breakdown, and staying up very late were catching up with Killian. He let loose a long and loud yawn. His eyes became heavier and heavier until sleep overtook him. His head slumped to his chest. He jerked awake some fifteen minutes later feeling a little refreshed. The wonderful images of last night ran though his head. He was surprised about dozing off despite the strobe lights flashing brightly in his eyes.

Way too late a night. I definitely need more sleep. At least I finally was able sleep after Gill stopped snoring.

[~]

"Oh, for the love of God," Killian screamed at the top of his lungs. "Stop your snoring, and for the sake of Mother Earth, shut the hell up," The snoring stopped, and Killian walked toward his bed.

Gill quietly laid in his tent the rest of the night.

Laying his head down on his pillow, Killian said, "Peace at last, peace at last."

The stars were soon replaced by the morning sunrise as Killian awoke, still sleepy. Gill still lay in his tent. Killian quickly decided to pack his gear and leave Gill, but not until he cleaned up Gill's mess. Hiking back to the parking lot, Killian saw only the SUV in the parking lot. Ecstatic, Killian thought, At least I have a ride. I couldn't stand listening to his voice, I'm glad I left. He'll talk himself to death before I go hiking with him again. One day with him was one day too many.

Killian checked out at the trail register. Finding the keys, Killian unburdened his back by throwing his pack into the rover, ending the long weekend of hiking. The drive out of the woods was challenging. The rover stalled numerous times, frustrating Killian. Shifting so he could restart the engine was harder than he expected. Luckily he made it out to Route 30, but the engine whined in protest as Killian tried to pick up speed. After a few miles, a loud bang resonated throughout the interior. At first Killian thought one of the tires had blown, but the SUV wasn't pulling to one side. Quickly he realized the engine was revving faster and faster, but the rover was coasting to a stop. "Just great! This ruins a perfectly good weekend," Killian yelled to himself.

[~]

"Sir, please step out of the vehicle," commanded the deputy sheriff.

Awakened from his thoughts, Killian saw the deputy standing next to the driver's window. He replied in a groggy voice, "Excuse me. What did you say?"

"Sir, please step out of the vehicle, with your hands in sight, now," the deputy repeated.

"Why?" Killian replied. He looked around the rover and noticed a state trooper outside the passenger's door.

"I want to talk with you," responded the deputy.

"When will the..."

"The tow truck will be here soon. Please step out of the vehicle," responded the officer.

Killian complied and led the officers toward the rear of the vehicle. The deputy asked him the usual questions while the trooper watched a few paces back. Killian felt slightly uncomfortable when the trooper asked him for permission to search the vehicle, but without hesitation he allowed the trooper to search the rover.

The trooper took the keys from the ignition and un-locked the rest of the doors, while the deputy patted Killian down on his patrol car. Using his maglight, the trooper searched under, over, behind, and in every possible place a person could have hidden anything. Having cleared the front seats, he proceeded to examine the rest of the vehicle.

Upon opening the tailgate, the trooper noticed the backpack with a camp ax peeking out. After removing the leather sheath, the trooper examined the ax with a forensic eye. The trooper looked at the deputy sheriff and nodded.

The sheriff said, "Sir, about an hour ago two hikers found a body near Pillsbury Lake. I'm placing you under arrest on the suspicion of murder."

Killian gave them a deer-in-the-headlights look. He wanted to run, but couldn't get his legs to move. The deputy efficiently handcuffed Killian and placed him in the back of his patrol car. He wanted to struggle and protest but knew silence was better.

A rollback wrecker finally came, loaded the SUV onto its bed, and drove away.

Sitting dumbfounded in the back of the cruiser, Killian muttered, "My perfectly planned weekend was completely ruined. How can it be?"

All I needed to do was drive to Northville, drop the rover off, hike back to Gloversville, and get on the bus. It was a perfect plan. I've done it a dozen times before, and no one even knows about it until it's too late. I always come out on top. All I needed was to sign the Northville trail register, and I could've kept my perfect weekend streak going. At least they are taking that piece of garbage SUV away for me. Now that that vehicle doesn't run, it makes the environment so much better.

Killian yelled at the top of his lungs, "Next time I'll make sure my hiking partner doesn't drive a stick shift!"

Chapter Seven

[Life's A Journey]

The windshield wipers removed the growing collection of water droplets with a faint squeak, which was almost drowned out by the defroster blowing high heat to keep the inside windshield fog-free. The diesel engine purred along through the early morning fog.

Awake since five, the two brothers had been riding in a their Ford 350 Super Cab for nearly an hour-and-a-half. They ran into a fog bank when they crossed the park boundary just outside of Harrisville. Even with low-beam headlights, the two men could see only about fifty feet in front of the truck. Everything else was either illuminated fog white or pitch black. When the fog became thicker outside Cranberry Lake, the driver reduced his speed even more. The passenger asked, "Do you even know where the road is? Because I sure the hell can't see it."

When the truck finally reached Tupper Lake, it pulled into the parking lot of the Lumberjack Restaurant. The passenger quickly opened his door and headed in to use the restroom. Only 17, Christopher Alexander was a senior from Natural Bridge, a member of the local Four-H Club, and the sax player in the school band. His father and older brother considered him to be a scrawny, five-and-a-half foot tall weakling. He had short curly black hair and a bony face. This morning, he was wearing jeans, a faded Old Navy T-shirt, and an old pair of Dexter boots, which were mainly worn in the winter. His mother still considered him the baby of the family and had tried her best to protect him from the torture of his cousins when the family gathered for a reunion. He knew that the only reason she has babied him is because he has had asthma for most of his life.

His brother, six years older, got out of the truck with a quick hop to the ground missing the running boards completely. With his two hundred pound, five-foot, ten-inch frame, he was a natural to work road construction most of the summer. Leroy, named after his grandfather, had developed a golden upper body, now covered by a light-brown flannel, hunting shirt. A camouflage ball cap, with the slogan, "My best trade was my wife for a shot-gun," covered his short light brown hair. He wore a pair of camouflage hunting pants and his tan leather hunting boots. He turned around and, having just bought the truck, pushed the keyless entry to lock the truck. He was happy to have a day off from work, considering the last two months he'd put in 60-plus hours every week.

When he entered the Lumberjack, Leroy grabbed an empty booth while he waited for his brother to return from the restroom. The place was packed with people who were enjoying cups of coffee and talking among them-selves. This restaurant, unlike a chain restaurant, had the distinct flavor of the Adirondacks. All over the walls and ceiling hung saws and axes of all types, from one and two-man crosscuts to single and double-bladed axes. The waitress came over, filled Leroy's cup with coffee, said, "I'll be right with you sir," and quickly left for another table.

When Christopher arrived at the booth, he picked up the menu. "So where are we going?"

"A trail near Paul Smiths," replied Leroy without looking up from his menu.

"How long?"

"About a half an hour, give or take. I don't know why Mom insisted that I have to take you hiking. You've been out in the woods just as much as I have, if not more."

"Because if I break my neck while hiking alone and survive, Mom will surely kill me, but if you're with me, she'll kill you. That's why," replied Christopher with an amused smile.

The waitress returned and took their orders. Christopher ordered three pancakes, bacon, and orange juice. Leroy got three eggs sunny-side up, hash browns, Canadian bacon, and more coffee. They waited in silence for their breakfasts. Christopher was admiring the saws and axes throughout the restaurant. Within ten minutes they were served; Christopher was amazed that his cakes were as big as a standard serving plate.

"I hope you're going to finish eating them; it's going to be a long day," said Leroy, as he munched on his last piece of Canadian bacon.

"Yes, Mom, I will," Christopher replied without looking at his plate again for he was stuffed.

Leroy paid the bill, and they headed to the truck. They left Tupper and headed toward Saranac Lake on Route 3. Despite the fog, and with the sunrise only a few minutes old, Leroy stayed at the speed limit for most of the way. He slammed on the brakes, almost missing the turn onto

Route 30, then headed north toward Malone. A half hour later the truck reached the small hamlet of Paul Smiths where they took a left turn at the college onto a two-lane blacktop county road. Within a couple of miles this back road became dirt, and Leroy tried to avoid the large potholes and bumps, but failed a few times and almost jarred Christopher out of his seat. Driving slower now, Leroy saw the small sandy parking area and turned in. A New York State Department of Environmental Conservation sign said it was the parking area for the St. Regis Mountain trail.

"We're here?" Christopher asked.

Leroy parked, turned off the engine, and stepped out of the truck. Leroy quickly headed toward the brush along the side of the parking lot to relieve himself.

Christopher got out, stretched his back, and said, "God, it's quiet here. Where's the trail?" He looked at the grayish fog bank and observed, "I can't see anything in this stupid fog."

Leroy came back to the truck, opened the rear door on his side, and pulled out a small camouflage daypack. He grabbed his water-resistant camouflage jacket off the back seat, put it on, and zipped it halfway.

Christopher grabbed his brand new North Face daypack and his dark blue jacket off the back seat of the truck from his side. He carried them around the truck and set the daypack down on the ground. Throwing his jacket on, he bent down and unzipped the pack and pulled out his camera, an old Nikon 35 mm with interchangeable lenses. He was about to sling the camera around his neck when his brother said, "If you don't want that ruined, I'd keep it in your pack."

"I don't think the fog will hurt the camera," Christopher replied as he pulled his arm through the strap, so that the camera was tucked next to his chest.

"You remember when Dad spilled that can of soda over the keyboard last year?" Leroy grabbed a small box out of his jacket pocket, opened it, and pulled out a turkey call. He placed it in his mouth and gave a series of yelps.

"You're not going to use that all day, are you?" Christopher asked as he put the camera back into his pack.

"Yes, if you are going to take all day getting ready." Being a sportsman since he was old enough to fire a gun, Leroy had developed a good sense of direction, especially when he'd been to an area before.

Christopher fumbled around in his jacket pocket, removed his inhaler, took two puffs, and replaced it back in his pocket.

Leroy locked the doors to the truck and placed the keys in his front pants pocket. He turned around, looked into the grayish white beyond, and said, "Let's go."

They headed out into the stillness, the cold moist air feeling comfortable on their exposed skin. The boys followed the dirt road and Leroy said, "I was told that at the end of this road there was one of the last great camps of the Adirondacks. You can't enter it from this road because of a barred gate and a keypad."

The silence of the morning was broken by the sound of falling water as they crossed over a small bridge. They had walked on for another hundred and fifty yards when Leroy found the trailhead on the right-hand side of the road. Stepping onto the trail, Christopher immediately went to the registration box, opened the door, and grabbed the book.

"What are you doing?"

"Signing us in for our protection," Christopher said. "That's what the sign says to do, so I'm doing it." He opened the hard covered book, flipped to one of the back pages, and picked up the short pencil. He filled in a blank line with the proper information. Replacing the book and pencil, he closed the door and pointed to the signs on the registration box, "Are you prepared to stay out all night?"

"No," his brother replied with an irritated tone. "Are you ready?"

"So, are we prepared?" asked Christopher as they crossed the footbridge.

"Prepared for what?"

"Staying out all night."

"I'm not planning on staying out all night," Leroy said shaking his head. "That's for the idiots that have never been in the woods and have no experience outdoors."

Leroy knew he had better pay close attention to the trail and to Christopher, because he knew that Christopher would get them lost. When they had played behind their house when they were younger, Christopher was notorious for getting lost in the woods. All he had to do was take a few steps off a well-marked path, and he would be utterly lost! Leroy still couldn't believe his brother had wanted to go hiking, because he knew that Chris could get lost even on this simple trail. That was why their mother insisted on Leroy's taking Christopher hiking.

The trail quickly ascended a small hill and started to meander through a forest of pine and beech. It skirted around a small watering hole and down into a small dale. As they started to ascend the next hill, the forest changed from a grayish white mass into a white blanket, with only the trees visible within thirty feet. The path followed an old logging road and leveled out when they passed next to a large rock face. They could see the water dripping from the moss and little plants growing from the cracks. The trail was muddy and slippery in some spots as it veered off the old logging road.

Christopher kept up with his brother's pace but was starting to get winded. He wasn't sure how much longer he could keep this pace and didn't want to slow his brother.

The fog deposited water onto the leaves, which eventually created large raindrops that fell throughout the forest. Some of the falling drops would trigger more drops to fall, creating a small rainstorm that could drench anyone standing under it. Leroy brushed too close to a sapling and got wet, but by this time he was drenched with sweat from hiking. The cool water felt nice on his exposed skin.

The path continued to meander through the woods, traveling around sides of hills, down into shallow valleys, and up onto rock outcroppings. They passed by boulders that were two to three times the size of their four-wheelers back home. They climbed over and under a couple of trees that had fallen across the path.

As Christopher was climbing up a very short but steep section, about a five-foot climb of moss and mud-covered rock, he slipped, fell onto his chest and slid back to the base of the rock.

Leroy asked, "Are you all right?"

"Fine. Lost my footing. I've hurt myself more shaving," said Christopher, wiping mossy mud off his pants.

Leroy said, "You're lucky that you didn't have your camera out. You might've broken it."

"Yeah, you're right," replied his brother.

"Why did you bring your camera with you anyways? You haven't even taken a picture."

"I haven't found anything to take a picture of," his brother replied as he scaled the slippery face.

"Doesn't look like you're going to get any really good pictures today."

Christopher shrugged and kept climbing in reply.

Crossing a relatively flat trail section, which passed through a forest of hardwoods, they sidestepped the muddier spots. After fifteen minutes of hiking, the trail started to roll, and they crossed over a few small dry streambeds that ran downhill from the mountainside, which was now on their right. The two brothers heard a bubbling stream off to their left and crossed it by walking over a footbridge.

Christopher was panting heavily and sat on a small boulder along the trail. He pulled out a water bottle from his backpack and took a couple of gulps between his heavy breathing. He handed the half-filled bottle to his brother.

Leroy said, "God, I could go for another cup of coffee right about now." He finished off the bottle of water by himself and said to his brother, "You gonna make it?"

Christopher nodded as he attempted to slow his breathing, getting his lungs full of air as he tried to prevent an asthma attack. After a few moments, Christopher could breathe easier and said, "I think you picked up the pace back there."

"Well, it's all uphill from here," Leroy replied.

"Uphill?" Christopher said as his jaw dropped, then looked at his feet and mouthed, "Oh my God."

Leroy just looked at his brother with a grin across his face and said, "Yeah, we're finally at the base of St. Regis.

The trail follows the stream a bit. It's another mile to the top." Leroy pointed up the trail to an unseen destination.

"Another mile!"

"You want to turn back now?" Leroy asked. After a few seconds of silence he said, "You know, Coach Smith's favorite expression was, 'You did all those so you can do the last one right.' So let's get going, if you're not going back to the truck."

"I'm glad I didn't have Coach Smith for any classes," responded Christopher as he placed his empty bottle inside his pack.

"The trail will be slippery as we go up, so watch your step and be careful."

The fog was dissipating, and the two brothers could see about two hundred feet. They started to ascend the trail with the stream on their right. The trail became steep, and Leroy outpaced Christopher, who had to stop climbing to catch his breath on multiple occasions. Leroy just kept on without looking back, and Christopher lost sight of his brother. Leroy sat down on a fallen tree while listening for a response from his turkey call, but he heard no calls. When Leroy saw his brother again back down the trail, he called out, "You O.K?"

"Yeah," Christopher said and then rested for a few minutes as Leroy headed on without saying another word. Christopher was able to keep up on this section of flat trail, but the trail took a sharp right turn and began to climb. His brother quickly started to outpace him again.

When Leroy was about fifty yards ahead of his brother, he turned around and yelled back, "I'll meet you at the top; take your time." He turned around and continued up the mountain.

Christopher struggled to climb the mountain. The higher he climbed, the steeper the slope became. The number of steps he took lessened while his resting time grew and grew. The trail entered the ravine that the two brothers had crossed at the bottom of the mountain.

Christopher arrived at a point where the trail squeezed between a boulder and the ravine wall. He stopped to suck in some air and without thinking he said, "Well, hi there."

Sitting on a small rock in front of the boulder was a man who turned toward the struggling hiker and replied in a quiet craggy voice, "Hi there back."

The man sitting on the rock was wearing a granite gray jacket and pants that blended with the rock behind him. A few strands of salt and pepper hair stuck out from under the hood of his jacket. The oversized hood hid his eyes, but the visible features looked like he had mountain ranges for wrinkles. The veins on the back of his hands looked like flowing rivers running from his fingertips to his wrists. On his lap rested a small white pipe with a matching white stem.

"Looks like you're having a hard time," said the old man, turning back to his lap and not looking at the anguish in the young man's face.

"Yeah," Christopher replied with a ragged breath. "This is my," a pause to catch his breath, "first time hiking here," another breath, "and I don't think," a wheezing breath, "I'm going to make it up," a struggling breath, "this damn mountain." Christopher gasped as he dropped his backpack on the ground.

The old man didn't say a word as he turned to look at the younger man.

"Do you know how much," a short pause, "further it is to the top?" Christopher asked as he finally began to catch his breath.

"Not much further, about four, maybe five hundred yards," replied the old man. "But there is still about a hundred feet of climb left."

Christopher couldn't believe it. "Ah, great. Why in the hell did my brother bring me up this particular damn mountain?" Christopher started to get pissed off at his brother, who was probably already at the top relaxing. The old man had turned back to the rock face and sat quietly staring at it.

Without looking at the young man, the elderly man said, "Why are you trying to run up St. Regis? St. Regis is not a running mountain." He looked at Christopher, "You don't look like a runner. You're not in shape even to be a hiker. Why do you think I'm sitting here?" Pointing to the ground below him. "If I had more room, I'd offer up a seat."

"I'm fine, thanks for asking," Christopher replied.

"Name's Doran K. Rapakid," said the old man as he picked up his pipe and placed it between his teeth.

"Christopher," he said as he shifted his weight from his right foot.

"So why are you running up this mountain?" Doran asked again.

"Well, I'm trying to keep up with my brother. I want to get to the top before he decides to start back down."

"I've seen a great many of hikers in my days, and there are two distinct types. I call one group the `baggers' and the other group the `explorers,' and you, my friend, are not a bagger," Doran told Christopher with a smile forming across his face.

"What do you mean by `baggers' and `explorers'?" Christopher looked confused.

The old man looked straight into Christopher's eyes. "Well, all hikers want to reach their goals, whether to see a mountaintop or a waterfall. A bagger hiker is a person that has so-called blinders on and can only see the trail, and they race to the top to bag the mountain, so to speak. A person who is an explorer will take their time and look beyond the trail to discover the surroundings that they will encounter along their journey. To me, your brother is a bagger, considering he passed me without even saying a word. Whereas you, you look like you're trying to become a bagger, but I don't think you can be one." A pause. "You're on the fence, and if you try to become a bagger, you will not succeed in your goal."

Doran thought for a few minutes and finally asked, "What do you see when you look at this massive slab of stone?" He pointed to the exposed surface of granite.

"All I see is a rock," the young man replied looking more confused than before.

"Well, I see George," replied the old man.

"George who? Where?"

Doran carefully took his pipe out of his mouth and used the pipe's stem like a pointer, "Well, the overhang looks like his forehead and underneath his forehead, that lighter colored oval area, that's his eye. And, of course, here's his nose," the old man was pointing to the ten-foot high exposed rock face. The top of the rock was the side of the mountain with a tree sticking out from the edge. There were lichens that had formed the discoloration in the rock.

"I still don't see this face you're referring to."

"Well, you're too close. Take a few steps back so you can get the bigger picture," Doran said.

Christopher turned and walked four steps down the mountain trail. He stopped, turned back to the old man, and then looked at the rock wall. Just as quick as he turned, the face in the rock popped out at him, and he said, "Oh my god, I can see it now!" A grin formed on his face from ear-to-ear, and all the pain in his lungs and legs just washed away. "I've got to take a picture of this!" He exclaimed as he unzipped his backpack. After a moment of fiddling with his camera, he took a picture of the face.

"Now, do you see the difference between the two types of hikers? One can only see the end results and would pass this rock without seeing the rock as it should be. The other would see the face in the rock and everything else that can be found along the trail. In turn they will find new experiences along the entire trip," Doran said.

"Yes, I do," exclaimed Christopher.

"Well, congratulations. You're now becoming a real explorer... if you don't put that camera back into your pack."

With a moment of hesitation Christopher said, "But I don't want to ruin it in the fog or break it if I fall."

"Don't worry about the fog, it won't hurt the camera. It'll burn off in about half an hour. If you fall and ruin the camera, well, that's an experience that you will just have to live with."

Lifting his backpack to his shoulders, Christopher then threw his left arm through the camera strap so that the camera's body would rest next to his chest. "Well, it was nice meeting you. Thanks for showing me George."

"You're welcome," Doran replied.

"See you at the top," Christopher said as he stepped through the rocks and headed to the top of the mountain.

Even with the extended rest, Christopher had to stop three more times before the trail finally leveled out. With the gentler slope he was able to finish without stopping as the trail rounded the backside of the mountain. Christopher climbed the last bit of trail on exposed rock. He saw his brother sitting on top of a boulder, looking out into the foggy sky beyond the mountaintop. On the far side of the exposed mountaintop was an abandoned fire tower.

"About time you got up here. What did you do, stop for a coffee break?" Leroy said in a very cheerful tone, "If you did, I hope you brought me some."

"I didn't think this trail would be so damn steep. I had to stop about a hundred times coming up," said Christopher, catching his breath. "I even talked to some old guy along the trail."

"What? You actually passed an old guy? I sure the hell didn't see anyone else," replied his brother.

"Well, hopefully he'll make it up here. I was impressed that he got up that far," Christopher said as he dropped his pack next to his brother's.

"Where did you see this guy?" Leroy asked, as if he didn't believe his brother.

"You know, where the trail passed next to the face," replied Christopher.

"What face?" asked his brother.

"The face is on the left where the trial squeezes past a rock wall and boulder. He was sitting below the boulder on the right-hand side of the trail," explained Christopher.

"It wasn't that foggy out, and I sure didn't see a face on a rock or a person sitting next to the trail. I think you're hallucinating from lack of oxygen," Leroy chuckled at his younger brother.

"Well, that old man said you wouldn't have seen the face anyways, and that you're a bagger."

"I've no clue what you're talking about. Are you ready to leave? My sore ass is getting wet," Leroy stood.

"Never mind; you just wouldn't really understand," replied his brother as he lifted his camera off his neck.

"Well, I see that you brought out your camera. Is it ruined yet?"

Turning his back to his brother, Christopher said, "No. If you want to leave, then go. I'm planning on taking more pictures and relaxing for a while."

"I don't know what you're going to take pictures of. The entire place is encased in fog. All you're going to get are white pictures," replied his brother as he stood on top of the lone boulder that was the highest point of the mountain.

Christopher started to walk around the exposed mountaintop, looking at the plants and trees that were growing in the crags of the rocks. He examined the abandoned fire tower to see if he could climb it, but decided that it was unsafe to climb the outside steel frame to get onto the second level of wooden steps. About fifteen minutes after arriving on top of the mountain, the sky brightened considerably and even the forest and ponds below could be seen. In patches the fog was lifting off the forest. Within the next ten minutes blue sky started to appear above Christopher's head, and in the distance to the east Whiteface could be seen clearly. Snapping pictures of the views from the top, Christopher finally ran out of film and had to go back to his pack to reload his camera.

As Christopher closed the back of his camera, he noticed another hiker clearing the tree line and approaching the two brothers. The newcomer was wearing a red jacket and blue jeans and said, "Morning."

Leroy returned the pleasantry and walked over to his backpack.

The newcomer looked around the top of the mountain and started to climb up on top of the boulder Leroy had just left.

"Did you see an elderly guy anywhere along the climb up here?" Christopher asked.

"I haven't seen anyone on the trail until I saw you guys. Sorry."

"Come on, let's go," Leroy said as he grabbed his backpack and started to head down the mountain. Christopher quickly gathered his pack and camera and followed his brother. When they were out of earshot of the hiker, Leroy said to his brother, "I told you there wasn't anyone on the trail. You were just hallucinating, but don't worry about it. If we spot him lying on the trail dead, then we can worry about it. O.K., let's go."

When the two brothers came upon the face, Christopher explained again what had happened and showed his brother the face in the rock, but Leroy still couldn't see it.

Leroy shook his head in disgust at his brother for wasting time and continued to insist his brother had hallucinated from lack of oxygen.

The way back to the truck was uneventful, and Christopher finished off another roll of film. He couldn't find any trace of the elderly man whom he had met on the slopes of St. Regis, but he did find several plants that looked very similar to the pipe he had held.

Chapter Eight

[Decisions]

"I know what I'm doing," Ozzy said to himself as he left the Garden parking lot. "I can't believe he thinks that I'm so inept…giving me the emergency contact number." Shaking his head in disbelief and stuffing the piece of paper in his jacket pocket, Ozzy started his daylong hike on the Southside Trail toward Johns Brook Lodge.

With a crystal clear sky filtering through the bare trees along the trail, the lodge wasn't Ozzy's final destination of the day, but the warm air and beautiful scenery made today one of the most perfect days anyone could hike in the Adirondack Mountains.

Ozzy to most everyone, Oswald to a select few, was six-feet tall and weighed in at a scant one-fifty. Dressed in his favorite hiking clothing, a pair of dark green nylon pants and white cotton long-sleeved shirt with a light gray wool sweater, Ozzy was comfortable this early spring day. Wraparound shades covered his brown eyes while short, dark, curly hair covered half his head; the rest had fallen out in his twenties. He carried his daypack with all the hiking essentials, including a set of snowshoes, strapped to the back. In each hand he had two trek poles, which were not necessary on the flat trail. In his opinion the best job in the world was his, a freelance writer, because he could create his own schedule.

When he looked outside this morning and saw the beautiful sunrise and clear blue sky, then felt the cool brisk temperature, Ozzy felt the "blocks" rising like the sun. Jen, his wife, started calling Ozzy's writer's block the "blocks" because they happened so frequently on days like this. When the radio weather forecaster said sixty by noon the "blocks" had definitely formed in his mind. All he could think about was leaving their Saratoga Springs home and heading to the mountains where he would become inspired to write. At breakfast Ozzy said, "Jen, I feel a serious case of the 'blocks' coming over me."

Jen replied, "Fine, just make sure you drop the kids off at school, and take the dog to the vet for his rabies shot."

By the time he got back from the vet, it was nearly nine. He excitedly changed his clothes, grabbed his gear, and got into his car. As he put the key into the ignition, he realized he didn't leave a note as to where he was going, so he quickly went back into the kitchen. Luckily his "blocks" allowed him to write on a post-it note. "Big Slide and the Brothers. Back around eight." He stuck his note on the fridge alongside all the other notes.

The north lane of the Northway was virtually empty as Ozzy cruised toward the Adirondacks. The balmy spring temperature was creeping up so Ozzy rolled down his VW

Jetta's windows to enjoy the fresh clean air. Listening to classical music from the local public radio station, Ozzy's drive to the Garden parking lot was very relaxing. As he pulled into the parking lot, Ozzy saw only a handful of cars, probably because it was a weekday and early spring. More hikers would start to arrive around Memorial Day. This was how he liked to hike, him and nature alone together.

After hiking a mile toward Johns Brook Lodge and the Interior Outpost, he started to relax, soaking in the beautiful serenity of the surrounding woods. The trail was muddy in spots, but with careful stepping, the mud could be avoided. Most of the snow had melted within the last few weeks but there was still plenty in the shadier areas. All the trees in the valley were budding while the spring sap run was nearing an end.

Reaching Johns Brook Lodge and the Interior Outpost was quite easy, considering the trails that lay before him. With the spring sun high above him, he stopped for lunch and thought, which direction should I take? Climb

Big Slide and then the Brothers, or climb Yard, over to Slide and then the Brothers? The peacefulness of the surroundings ended when three hikers approached the lodge from the Hopkins Trail direction.

The three hikers stopped for a water break and to light up cigarettes. Ozzy extended his water break until the three hikers started out again and turned onto the trail to Big Slide. Instantly he thought, Damn, I don't want to trek behind those smoke addicts. That smell! I don't want to breathe that crap. I want clean air. They're just going to ruin my day of hiking. If I follow them, knowing me, I'll catch them at a smoke break, and I'm going to gag for the rest of the hike. I won't be able to pass them on the trail either because they'll try to stay in front of me. How am I going to get over my writer's block this way?

Ozzy stood still for a few minutes more and said to himself, "Returning home seems plausible, man. But I came all this way to climb at least one mountain today."

He thought for a while. What to do? "I don't want to climb Yard again, but I really don't want to see those guys, so climbing Yard could be worth it."

They could hike from Big Slide to Yard, which means I would see them. An idea struck him like a lightning bolt. What about going to climbing Upper Wolf Jaw and Armstrong? I haven't done those yet. A grin formed ear-to-ear as he sprinted to the trail.

The Range Trail started out dry with mud in several places. It turned to mud and flowing water, eventually becoming hard-packed snow and ice. The higher the trail climbed, the more snow was on the path, waiting to be melted by the sun. The trail was easy to follow because it became a foot deep, hard-packed snowshoe trail.

Hmm, should I get my snowshoes on, even though I'm not postholing yet? He asked himself.

Bare booting the snow-packed trail supported Ozzy's weight without his sinking more than an inch into the ice-covered snow. If I put them on, I will slow down. When I start to break the trail, I'll get them on. He went on climbing bare boot.

As Ozzy climbed, the air temperature slowly dropped into the lower forties. At the trail junction of Upper and Lower Wolf Jaw, Ozzy was sweating profusely so he removed his soaked sweater. Immediately a chill passed over him. While grabbing some water and a snackbar, he examined the trail map, and he thought, while I'm here, why don't I climb Lower Wolf Jaw as well? It's only a half a mile climb.

"Not a bad idea. I would say," he responded.

After a steep ascent and finding the lookout on top of Lower Wolf Jaw, Ozzy rewarded himself with water and a power bar. That's number twenty-nine, just seventeen more to go. Hurray! Only staying fifteen minutes on top, he headed back down the trail from which he came to tackle Upper Wolf Jaw (and number thirty) next.

The perfectly blue sky was covered in cirrocumulus clouds. In the western skies of the Adirondacks a grayish white cloud bank moved closer to the High Peaks. Ozzy paid little heed to the developing weather.

Having had practice skiing with snowshoes before on steep slopes and fearing an uncontrolled slip and fall on the descent, Ozzy left his snowshoes in place as he headed down the mountain. The snow pack on the trail started to soften. Ozzy's boot frequently broke through the crusty layer, and his leg sank to mid-calf. Even using the trek poles, the postholing upset his balance, and he fell down twice before he got back to the Range Trail junction.

At the trail junction Ozzy looked at his watch, saw that it was twenty minutes to three, and exclaimed, "Damn, time flies when you're having fun. I better press on."

The Range Trail was still solid since it ascended the northern face of Upper Wolf Jaw, making the journey easy. Near the top the trees once again thinned as the trail started to soften. The western clouds grew closer, even starting to block the sun for minutes at a time. With the clouds, the breeze became windy. Ozzy shivered and donned his sweater when he stopped at the top of Upper Wolf Jaw for a water break. The air temperature was dropping quickly, so before he continued, he brought out his heavy jacket, a woolen hat, and gloves from his pack and put them on. He felt the results quickly.

The climb up "thirty" was easy compared to other High Peaks climbs he'd already accomplished. The descent conditions of Upper Wolf Jaw were similar to Lower Wolf Jaw's softening snow and ice pack, but this time Ozzy un-packed his snowshoes so he could try and pick up his pace. In some places it didn't help as he sunk hip deep into snow and had to climb out. When he reached the col between Armstrong and Upper Wolf Jaw, the sun had disappeared, and within moments the snow started flying.

The snowflakes startled Ozzy, but he went on with climbing Armstrong. As more and more flakes fell, he thought, where in the hell did this snow come from? I've got to make it over Gothic so I can get thirty-one, but if this weather turns any nastier I have no choice. I'll have to turn around. Cresting Armstrong, Ozzy continued toward Gothic without a momentary pause.

The High Peaks disappeared, followed by the stunted conifers. The fresh snow started to pile, and blowing white was all Ozzy could see. The old snowshoe trail was the only thing that kept Ozzy on track, and even that was quickly filling in with drifting snow. I've come too far; turning back isn't an option. I've got to push on.

Climbing Gothic, Ozzy struggled to progress. One more step. A breath. Just one more step. A breath. His thoughts repeated with each step. Breaking a new trail knocked what little strength he had left. Fatigue set in, and he labored to lift his dead legs out of the fresh snow. Every step ahead only gained him a few inches because his foot slid backward in the fresh snow on the steep slope.

Gale-force winds gusted over the mountain, the temperature plummeted into the low teens, and the snow intensified. Ozzy yelled out, "What happened to my warm and beautiful day? I'm in a damn whiteout!"

As the sunset and the whiteness became darkness, Ozzy struggled to summit Gothic. Stopping for a brief second, Ozzy took off his pack and dug out his headlamp, placed it over his woolen hat, and turned it on. A beam of light pierced the snowy darkness about ten feet in front of him. He continued the slow progression up the slope.

When the trail finally leveled, Ozzy said to the wind, "Finally! I think I've made it to the top of Gothic." There were no landmarks for him to be sure, and Ozzy quickly got disoriented. He tried to follow the trail down the south side of the mountain. He paused for a moment when he realized the futility of following an unseen, buried trail. In this weather if I choose a random direction, I'll never find the trail.

Once again Ozzy started to remove his pack, but a gust of wind caught him, and he lost his balance. He fell in the powdery snow and started to slide down the long slope. After coming to a rest he thought, luckily I didn't slide off the mountain. Lying there peacefully in the snow, he caught his breath as more snow fell onto his face and slowly filled in around him.

I need to get up, before I'm buried in the snow.

"Let me rest, this is so peaceful, and I'm so tired. I just want to lay here forever in this fresh fallen snow." He started to shiver.

He laid there forever.

Getting up with snowshoes was difficult. He tried to lift himself with his poles, but he could only lift his body a foot when his arm strength gave out. Falling back into the snow, he created a deeper body impression. The only way I'm going to get up is if I take my snowshoes off. The snowshoe straps were difficult to loosen, but he eventually removed the snowshoes. Standing in the fresh snow, he only sank to boot deep, but he had to wipe the snow from his face and headlamp.

"If I had a compass right now I could get off this blasted mountain, but, ah hell, I just remembered that my compass is always in Jen's pack," Ozzy said.

I need to put my snowshoes back on before I'm buried here, his mind told him.

Bent over to tighten the snowshoe straps, his left arm brushed his jacket pocket, where he felt something solid and rectangular. After finishing with his snowshoes, he ungloved his hand, and, using his very cold fingers, searched his pocket. He pulled out the treasure and looked at it, a compass. Well, how in the hell did that get in there? I don't remember putting it in, Jen must have. Throwing off the pack, he rummaged though one of the side pockets and withdrew a map of the High Peaks. Unfolding the map was difficult in the blowing snow; his fingertips were numbing, but he gripped the map firmly. Struggling with the compass, the map, the wind, and the headlamp, he tried to determine the trail location. Without warning, a gust of wind grabbed the map, and in a fraction of a second, he lost sight of it as it disappeared into the darkness beyond. Instinctively he threw the compass, trying to stop the map from blowing away, but the compass disappeared into the snow and darkness as well.

He sat in the dark. "I'm not going to find that map."

It's probably in Vermont by now. He chuckled.

"I'm not getting out of here tonight. That's for sure," he shook his head.

I'd better start fixing a shelter before I freeze to death. Once daybreak comes, I'll be all right and I'll hike out. A cold shiver ran down his spine.

Using one of the snowshoes as a shovel, he dug in the snow where he had fallen. Minutes passed, and the hole got deeper. His heart pounded, his arms and legs hurt. His body shook ever so slightly. The deeper he tunneled, the warmer he felt as winds howled outside. After twenty long and exhaustive minutes, the snow cave was done. He closed the entrance with his snowshoes. The headlamp illuminated his breath as the air inside warmed slightly.

Exhausted, he laid in the snow cave for an eternity. His body started to shake uncontrollably. Fire. I need to get warm before hypothermia fully sets in.

Searching his pack, he retrieved his Whisperlite camp stove and fuel bottle and set it up. With the stove all primed and ready to go, he remembered the most critical part, a lighter. He searched his pack three times trying to find anything that would light the stove. "I've got my matches in here somewhere." The search went from his pack to his jacket and pants pockets. With no hope of find anything to light the stove; he pounded his fist into the snow next to him. "C-c-calm down, calm down," he said.

He tried to relax and think where the matches were, but soon he resumed the desperate search of his pack, his pockets, and the snow cave floor. After twenty solid minutes he stopped from exhaustion and disorganization.

Shivering overtook his struggle to obtain heat.

Where in the hell did I leave my matches?

"I-I-I packed them," he yelled as he shook his head. Calmer, he said, "I packed them. I placed them next to-o-o the water bottles-s-s last night." He waited for a response.

I know I placed them on the table next to my water bottles. I have my water bottles, but I can't believe I left them there.

"I wouldn't mind-d-d a flint and steel right now." His shoulders slumped and his head hung low as he grew despondent in the small snow cave.

In the cramped quarters he sat on his empty pack to conserve his body heat, even as his shivering grew more violent. Too tired to pick up his stuff strewn about the cave, he noticed something that wasn't there before: a small, hard plastic, liquid-filled container. Taking off his right glove, he picked up the little rectangular object and, in the full light of his headlamp, saw a new cigarette lighter with a clear red plastic body. He said. "I-I-I don't remember packing this, but-t-t right now I don't mind-d-d."

My sweet dear Jen packed it. Light the camp stove before you freeze to death, idiot.

His numb fingers fumbled with the lighter, using his left hand to place it in his right palm so his thumb was on the striking wheel. He pulled down to light. Nothing happened. Several more tries gave the same result. The lighter fluid is too cold, put it inside your jacket. After a few moments of waiting, he tried to get a flame, but none appeared. After checking to see if the valve was open, he tried again. Pulling down on the striker wheel so hard he felt the striker wheel's grooves grate his numb thumb, a snapping sound echoed in the snow cave.

He examined the lighter. It looked fine. He tried again, but this time the striker wheel didn't move. Turning the lighter over to examine it further, the striker wheel fell out. Ozzy's mouth dropped as he watched the striker wheel disappear into the snow.

"Crap-p-p! I can't believe my luck-k-k." He shook his head in complete, utter disbelief.

Not finding matches, Ozzy had known he was in trouble, but the broken lighter meant serious trouble. Without fire he couldn't dry out, warm up, or boil water for his instant soup. To survive the night, he needed to stay warm and replenish his energy. If he ate and rested, he knew he could hike to the Interior Outpost come daylight.

Opening the instant soup package, he looked at the stiff noodles, broke a bite off and stuck it in his mouth. His mouth was drier than the snow, so he grabbed for a water bottle. Inside the bottle was a solid block of ice. He spit the noodles out and tossed the bottle toward his feet.

Suddenly he found two frozen candy bars and took a bite. Ozzy heard a crunch. A razor-sharp pain radiated from his jaw. He spit the mashed candy bar out. Along with the candy there was a trail of blood. He probed his mouth with his tongue and felt his two front teeth missing.

Shaking uncontrollably, he curled up into a tight fetal position, trying to conserve what little body heat he had left. Lying in the cave, the shaking not stopping, he fumbled with the jacket zipper to reveal soaked clothing underneath. He undressed down to his underwear, everything else was soaked. Feeling warmer, he stopped searching for dry clothes, but the shaking continued.

Ah, I'm warming up already. Now why didn't I do this before? It feels like summer in my nice warm cave.

"You-u-u put on-n-n dry clothes," he said, examining the littered floor for dry clothing.

Without heat, I can't get warm and have a hot meal. I can't stop shivering.

"Y-Y-You-u-u st-st-stop-p-p sh-sh-shivering."

Looking through his possessions, he uncovered his light gray wool sweater. He grabbed the sweater and held it next to his face to feel the soft dry wool. It's soaked. It won't keep me warm. I can't wear it.

In the snow cave, Ozzy was numb to the outside world, not caring about the snowstorm, food, water, or even warmth anymore. He stopped shivering. When I get home I'm going to write the best survival story anyone has ever written about the most perfect day a hiker could have

[~]

Securing my lightweight backpack, I set out toward the trailhead to the Johns Brook Lodge when a New York State Forest Ranger stopped me and said, "Good afternoon, where are you headed? If you don't mind my asking."

"I'm going to JBL, then climb up Slide and then down the Brothers," I replied.

"That's quite a hike for a late start. Can you complete the trip before sunset?" the ranger asked bluntly.

"Yeah, I've done it before, besides I'm prepared for anything," I told him, confident in my own abilities.

"Do you have winter gear in your pack right now? Even though it's sixty degrees and sunny right now, there's a major winter storm racing here, and storm warnings have already been posted for the mountains tonight through morning with two feet of new snow possible. The temperatures are going to be dropping into the teens over night." The ranger stated, trying to frighten me into not going.

Curing my writer's block was more important to me than a little snow, so I said, "I'll be out and heading for home before it starts to snow on Mount Marcy."

"Just in case, here is my cell phone number." The ranger handed me his business card and said his goodbye and good luck. He headed toward his Jeep to report back to headquarters for shift change.

I headed down the Southside trail, completely passing the trailhead register. I never looked back. Mistake One: Sign in at the trail register.

[~]

Snapping out of his writing, he found his cell phone in his pocket. He turned it on and got a signal. Jen must be worried to death, I must call her and tell her I love her. He dialed the number, but got no answer. Call the ranger.

"Help. I'm stuck on Gothic," he said into the phone.

Overhead, a helicopter could be heard over the howling winds. A rescue party is looking for me. Ozzy broke out of the snow cave into the wind as he looked into the darkness beyond. The helicopter's noise grew louder than the wind. Searchlight sweeps passed him ten feet away. The helicopter moved on without a second pass.

"I'm here! Please, come back!" The wind swallowed his voice. "I'm here! Please, come back!"

Suddenly, a two-ranger rescue team appeared and found the nearly frozen body of Ozzy. After an extended stay in the hospital for exposure and frostbite, he slowly recovered at his home, sleeping peacefully each morning in his log cabin home. The fireplace was always blazing. The silk sheets wrapped around his body. He never wanted to get out of bed.

[~]

Weeks later, Joel and Brandon were having fun sliding down the snow-covered slopes of Gothic. When they arrived at the tree line, Brandon's shirt caught on a long aluminum snowshoe. After uncovering their find, they realized that the snowshoe was still attached to the owner. The owner laid in a fetal position with his trek poles in-hand and his backpack still on. Joel and Brandon ran down the trail to Johns Brook Lodge to notify the search party they had found the missing hiker.

Chapter Nine

[Ice Fishing]

Since I own the only convenience store for twenty miles in any direction, many regular customers enter my store to buy their weekly gas and groceries. The off-season is usually slow; that is, I regularly get twenty customers a day, ten of whom are the permanent residents who live nearby, looking for the latest gossip from my wife. The rest fill up their gas tanks, grab a snack, and leave without saying a good-bye. And every once in a while I give directions to a lost tourist who's looking for a nearby town, a hidden road, or a local resident.

While I run the till, stock the shelves, and every once in a while pump someone's gas, the store manager, my wife Esther, runs the business, orders the stock, keeps the books and me in check. We've asked ourselves numerous times why we still stay open. Our profits are very small, and the competition is fierce, even though it's twenty miles away. The bank has come close to foreclosing on our house and store one too many times. But we always find the reasons and the money to stay open, because if we left our home, store, friends, and neighbors we would never feel happy again. We've just had too many wonderful experiences over the past fifty years growing up, living, and working in the Adirondacks.

When the black flies return to our mountains, like the swallows to Capistrano, so do the summer residents and tourists, who increase our business by 250 percent. Having worked in the store for so long, we are on a first name basis with many of the summer residents. We even have seen the second and third generations spending their summer vacations living here on the lakes, in the woods, and coming into our store.

Summer brings new arrivals our way all the time. Most only stay a week or two then head home, never to return to our neck of the woods. I've noticed that there are two types of tourists who don't return: those who don't appreciate the slower pace of life, and those who don't enjoy the real outdoors as much as they thought. Both types of tourists, in my opinion, don't open their minds to the unique folks and community that forms here from late spring to early fall.

On the other hand, those who return can make quite an impression on the community, like the two unforgettable customers I had last year. I will call these two guys "Blake" and "Allen," since I never got their names.

One early spring day, on which it was raining and snowing on the mountaintops, Blake and Allen entered the store. Blake, who entered first, was roughly six feet tall and weighed at least 220 pounds. His straight black close-cut hair was starting to gray around the temples. He wore a slate gray trench coat that matched his eyes. A shirt and tie poked out of the tightly closed coat, and a pair of newly shined shoes slapped the wood floor.

A few minutes later Allen entered the store. His dark hair and tan L.L. Bean jacket were soaked from pumping gas in the cold rain. A shiver ran down his six-foot, two-inch frame even though he was wearing a wool sweater underneath his jacket, making him look heavier than he really was. His blue jeans started to steam as water dripped off his leather hiking boots. His squarish face was clean-shaven except for the thick, neatly trimmed mustache.

Once Allen entered, Blake came over to the register and paid for the gas. Allen looked around the store, which of course didn't take long. Allen came over to Blake, pulled on his coat sleeve, and led him to the back of the store. I became suspicious of their actions and held my breath for a long moment. They stopped in front of the small assortment of fishing tackle on a back shelf. They quietly talked to one another until Allen piped up and asked, "Do you have any ice fishing equipment?"

I started to breathe again as I looked at them strangely. I knew trout season had only opened a week ago because I went fishing on opening day and didn't catch anything. But this strange question of ice fishing equipment blew my mind because the only safe ice available now would be on the small ponds in the High Peaks, which were dead from the acid rain. I responded, "I might have a few jigs and a tip-up in back, but I don't carry that much fishing equipment, even in summer. Would you like me to go in the back and look?"

Blake nodded.

Since Esther was at the cash register, gabbing on the phone, I walked back into the storeroom and rummaged around. I kept my ears open, and not finding any ice fishing gear, I quickly returned to the front and told the gentlemen my findings.

"We're just looking for some discounted gear, that's all," replied Blake. "Do you know where Pleasant Pond

Road is by any chance? We bought a camp and would like to see what we bought. Hopefully we'll be able to spend some quality time fishing there come this summer."

"Head north about two miles and the road is on the right. The camp you're talking about is a mile or so back in the woods. I wouldn't try driving back there though. If I were you, I'd park my car along the road and hike in. The camp road shouldn't be too hard to follow with the snow still on the ground."

They thanked me for the directions and said they'd see us in a month or two. As they drove away, I noticed that their red SUV was from the City. I said to my wife, "How much are you willing to bet that they'll be back here to call for a tow truck to pull them out?"

Either Esther didn't hear me, or she didn't want to comment. She just continued to talk on the phone.

With the warming sun of early June the summer residents arrived to enjoy their summer vacations. Blake and Allen arrived right alongside the vacationers. They entered the store just before closing one Friday night and bought food, beer, soda, chips, two poles, line, and a handful of jigs and lures.

Allen placed all of the items on the counter and asked, "Do you have any ice?"

"Outside to your left, past the stack of firewood. They're two dollars each," I said as I started totaling up the groceries. Esther bagged the food using four plastic bags.

"I'll take one please," Allen replied.

I added the ice to the total without a second thought.

"Take only what you bought, or I'll charge double next time," I stated as I finished ringing up Allen's bill.

Allen grabbed three of the grocery bags and headed toward the door, returning a few minutes later for the rest. Blake unloaded his arms on the counter, and I started to total his bill. He quickly headed back and added another armful of food and two more fishing poles. They were the biggest buyers of the day; the two bills totaled three hundred and twenty four dollars and ten cents, which they paid in cash. I was surprised that they didn't complain about the prices like most tourists who stop. They grabbed the rest of the groceries and headed out the door. Blake placed the groceries in the back of the SUV while Allen got a bag of ice from the freezer and placed it in a cooler. When they left, I locked up the store, and we headed to bed so we'd be ready for another early morning wake-up call.

The next afternoon Blake returned and bought a handful of lures, night crawlers, and hooks. He placed the items on the counter and said, "I'll take a bag of ice, too."

I rang up the total, which he paid for in cash, then left without saying another word. He grabbed the bag of ice as he left.

Over the next two weeks both men came into the store to buy different lures and jigs, one of every style, color, and size that I had in the store. Every so often they'd buy night crawlers or minnows. But every time they came in they bought a bag of ice. By the end of the first week of their buying spree I finally asked them, like I did most fishermen, "Any luck?"

Every time their response would be the same, "A few small ones." A shoulder shrug, "Haven't caught anything worth keeping though."

As the summer temperatures rose, the two men started coming into the store more frequently, but they kept to themselves. They still bought more lures, jigs, and bait. They even asked me if I could get some crawfish for them to try. I asked a local boy to catch a dozen crawfish from a local creek, and I paid him five dollars. The next day Blake and Allen came in to pick up the crawfish along with their regular purchase.

The difference in their buying habits was the ever increasing number of bags of ice they bought. At the start of summer it was two and three bags a day, but by the end of July they were buying ten to fifteen. During a really hot day they came into the store three times just to buy ice.

In the middle of a scorching August heat wave the summer vacationers started to complain about our lack of ice in the icebox. I asked the delivery driver to increase the number of bags and stops per day during the heat wave.

He said, "I can't spare a bag even if it would fit, and my route doesn't come back this way on my return."

Esther told me, "You'd better talk to those two men before the rest of the vacationers revolt and buy their groceries elsewhere. We need enough ice for everyone's beer, soda, and watermelon for the Labor Day weekend, or they'll go to Ted's store next year. Most people today don't care if they drive an hour to get groceries."

Days before the last big weekend, Blake and Allen came into the store for their weekly buying of groceries, worms, lures, and twenty bags of ice.

I told them, "I'm sorry but for the next week I'm limiting the number of ice bags purchased to two per day per customer."

Astonished, they couldn't believe what I said and insisted on buying twenty bags each.

Flabbergasted, I asked, "What do you need with forty bags of ice anyways?"

Blake replied, "It's hot out! We've fished all summer but we haven't caught any big ones yet." Shaking his head, "Just small ones every day. The small ones don't last long in this heat so we throw them back."

"We did catch one big one, but somehow it got off the stringer," replied Allen.

I was in shock and replied, "I've fished on that pond for years, and I know it has some big fish in it. With all the bait and tackle you two bought this summer, something should have bit. So you're telling me that you haven't caught a fish worth keeping all summer? Hell, I've left a bare hook in the water and caught something."

"Who said we're fishing for fish? We're fishing for ice," Blake said nonchalantly.

On hearing this, my jaw hit the floor! After recovering I said, "What in the hell are you talking about?"

"Yeah, this ice fishing season has been extremely lousy. I thought ice fishing in the Adirondacks would be better than our fishing trips to Minnesota. I've never seen so little action in my life. We must be on a dead pond or something," Allen replied as he paid for four bags of ice.

Bewildered at what they said, I told them with strong emotion, almost yelling at them, "First of all, you go ice fishing in the middle of winter when there's ice on the pond. You fish through the ice with tip-up and jig poles, not crank baits and worms. You don't go fishing for ice cubes in the middle of summer! Ice cubes melt, for Pete's sake, even the big ones."

Allen looked at me and said, "That sounds too dangerous and too cold." He paused, "Fishing on a frozen lake? You're nuts."

Blake said to Allen as they were leaving, "I think you're right. Next year we need to get a refrigerator with a freezer. It's a lot of work to keep our beer cold." A pause, "We should even get a built-in ice-cube maker so we could have the little half moon ice cubes. I think we'll be able to catch them better than the square ones we have now."

"I believe you're right," replied Allen.

That was the last time I saw them that summer. Now I'm waiting for them to show up with the rest of the summer residents. Hopefully they'll have better luck ice fishing this year.

Chapter Ten

[Snowy Mountain]

"In a cold November rain..." blasted from the radio alarm clock on a milk crate beside the bed.

"I hope it doesn't rain. I want snow," Mike said groggily as he turned off the radio. Lying in bed for a few more seconds so that his eyes could fully open after the long restful sleep, Mike threw the covers back and headed toward the upstairs bathroom. He walked quietly past his parents' bedroom, where one of them was snoring loudly. When he reached the bathroom, he quietly closed the door and turned on the light.

He was blinded, but awake. After recovering from his temporary blindness, he used the toilet and brushed his teeth. In the mirror he saw that his brown straight hair atop his boyish face needed to be tamed. His facial hair was still underdeveloped since he could hardly notice the two-day-old growth. His five-feet, eight-inch height gave him an edge in the 130-pound weight class for his high school wrestling team. His shirtless, thin upper body was nicely defined from all of the conditioning, and the three trophies he'd won this year proved it.

Mike headed toward his brother's bedroom. Opening the door, he reached for the light switch and toggled it rapidly. The strobe effect awoke his brother. Brandon rose like Frankenstein's monster. As the bedspread fell from his head, his hair looked like Albert Einstein's, standing straight out in tangles. Sleepily Brandon asked, "What?"

Mike responded quietly, not wanting to wake their parents, "Get up so we can get going."

"It's too damn early," replied Brandon as he fell back onto his pillows.

"I want to go before Mom and Dad wake up. Otherwise we will need to do chores, and we won't get to the top before sunrise."

"Fine," Brandon said as he threw off the covers and got to his feet.

Mike went back to his room to get dressed. He pulled his long underwear from the clean laundry pile that was on the floor next to his bed. After finding a pair of wool socks in his dresser drawer, he got a long-sleeved T-shirt and sweater from the closet. After looking everywhere, he remembered there was a pair of pants in the laundry basket in the hall. The jeans he found were still clean enough. He had only worn them yesterday.

Quietly descending the stairs, Mike found Brandon already dressed in the kitchen. Brandon was two years older and just as well built. He was the captain of the wrestling team, weighing in at 160 pounds. His brown hair was now tamed, and he was dressed similarly to his brother, Mike.

Brandon set out to prepare instant brown sugar oatmeal for both of them, all the while watching and waiting for the kettle of water to boil. He poured two large glasses of apple juice and set them next to the waiting bowls. When a faint whistle could be heard, Brandon pulled the kettle off the burner and poured the boiling water over the sweet smelling oatmeal.

While waiting for the oatmeal to cool, Mike rifled through the cupboards. He found two chocolate power bars in the pantry, grabbed two apples from the fruit bowl, and added two full water bottles from the refrigerator. He placed the goodies on the kitchen table for packing later.

Brandon was eating by the time Mike finished his treasure hunt. The brothers ate without saying a word. They knew what the day was going to bring them. When each was finished with breakfast, they rinsed their dishes and placed them in the dishwasher. Otherwise their mother would yell at them when they got home.

Mike glanced at the thermometer on the garage wall, noticed that it was nearly ten degrees Fahrenheit, and said, "It's going to be cold today."

"Yep," replied Brandon as he climbed the stairs once more to grab his pack.

Mike's daypack was laying next to the front door so he grabbed the power bars, apples, and water bottles from the table and stowed them in his pack. Retrieving a set of snowshoes and trek poles, one of his Christmas presents, from the living room, he placed them next to his daypack so that he could get dressed to head outside. From the front door closet he grabbed his green windbreaker jacket and pants. Next came his heavy ski jacket, with the old passes still attached to the zipper pull, and then finally he snagged a hat, hiking boots, and gloves.

Brandon quietly bounded down the stairs fully dressed, carrying his daypack and an older set of snowshoes to the front door.

Loaded with their gear, they headed outside toward Brandon's 1991 dark blue Pontiac Grand Am. A light dusting of snow covered the windshield. Mike made two portholes with his gloved hands, while Brandon popped the trunk. They loaded their gear and quietly closed the trunk.

The Pontiac's doors were unlocked since they lived in the middle of nowhere. It was as cold inside as it was outside. Last night while making his plan Mike decided to use his car for two reasons. One, it was the last car in the driveway, and two, he could pop the clutch and coast down the driveway until they were on the dirt road.

Once they were on the dirt road, Mike turned the key, and the engine fired up. The fan belt squealed loudly. The road was covered with a light dusting of snow. The road crews had not been out yet to lay down their daily coating of sand.

Since it had snowed for the past two weeks, the snow banks along the dirt road were nearly three feet high in places. Mike and Brandon loved the snow, never wanting it to melt until mid-April when trout fishing started. Then they were glad when the water temperature warmed up a few degrees.

As the sun rose over the distant mountains, highlighting the snow-covered trees, the two teens drove toward their destination. The drive seemed to take hours on the slippery back roads but eventually they made it safely to the parking lot of Snowy Mountain. The car tires crunched over the blanket of fresh snow.

They exited the car, and Mike opened the trunk. Strapping on their snowshoes was quick and easy, giving them flotation in the deep powdery snow that lay before them. Throwing on their daypacks, they readjusted the waist and chest belts so the daypacks fit securely on their backs despite all the extra clothing they had on.

At the trailhead they noticed no one had climbed the mountain since the last major snowstorm two days ago. The surrounding peaks were completely covered in snow. Fresh powder blew from one of the peaks, cascading through the cold air and landing gently on the mountain.

Brandon looked at Mike and asked, "You ready to tackle this beast?"

"As ready as I'll ever be," Mike replied as he started breaking the trail. Mike's first step went knee-deep into the snow, the same for the second. The tricky part was the third step: he lifted his foot out of the snowy hole and placed it in front of him. He almost lost his balance, but with the trek poles he was able to remain upright. Brandon had it easier following in Mike's steps. The hike to the base of the mountain was uneventful. It seemed to pass by quickly, despite having to break trail the entire way.

Surprised by how far his younger brother had broken the trail, though they were both very physically fit, Brandon asked before the ascent started, "Do you want me to break the trail for a while?"

"Yeah," Mike replied, slightly out of breath.

Brandon made his way around Mike and started the ascent. The trail quickly steepened, and soon both brothers started taking frequent breaks so that they could rest and catch their breath. Mike noticed that the trail was so steep that every step Brandon took forward, he slid back, making progress that much harder. During one of the short breaks he said, "We're going to have fun downhill skiing when we get back here."

"How can we downhill ski if we didn't bring skis with us in the first place?" asked Mike, looking confused.

"We're skiing with snowshoes," Brandon replied.

"But mine have crampons on the bottom," Mike responded, still looking confused.

Brandon, having more experience using snowshoes in the mountains, responded, "I think your brain is frozen, dear brother." A pause. "The snow is loose, and the trail is very steep so when we descend we're pretty much going to be downhill skiing whether we like it or not. Anyway, it's safer that way than falling on our butts and sliding uncontrollably down the mountain."

"Oh," replied Mike. "O.K. You're right. Let's move."

As they pushed onward, the sun warmed their backs even though the air was still cold. The two approached an east-facing ledge near the top. They made their way onto it after their long, exhausting journey. They took off their packs, extracted their water bottles, and then toasted one another as they celebrated the wonderful morning sunrise.

"Mike! Brandon! What the hell are you two doing up there?" their coach yelled from down in the parking lot. "Don't you know we have a tournament starting in two hours? I need you two to conserve all of your strength so we can win this tournament."

Brandon responded, "We're starting our warm-ups, Coach. We beat you here and figured the school was locked. And my car's heater sucks. So we figured we'd kill a few birds with one snowshoe trip."

"Well, get down here and take off your snowshoes before someone catches you up on that snow bank and gives me hell about it," replied the coach.

They both attempted to ski down the fifteen-foot high snow bank, but only made it ten feet before they had to walk. After removing their snowshoes and placing them in the trunk of Brandon's car, they headed in toward the locker rooms to get ready for the day's wrestling matches.

Chapter Eleven
[The Last Patrol]

Camping outdoors is a new experience every time a tent stake is hammered into the ground. Whether you're pitching a tent at a public campground with modern facilities or bivouacking in the middle of the wilderness with the ground as your bed and the stars as your blanket, there's no better feeling than considering yourself as a modern day explorer in one of the last surviving wildernesses of our world. Most camping trips are not dangerous to the camper, but they are filled with wonder and enjoyment to the explorers who dare to tackle these vast lands.

Two years ago, I was camping with two of my best friends, Peter and Mike, at Marcy Dam in the Adirondacks.

Peter and Mike are brothers separated by five years of age, but looking at them, most people would swear they were twins. They both have six-foot athletic frames and not an ounce of fat between them. They have curly jet-black hair cut in a flat top for the summer months, chiseled jaw lines, and bright blue eyes. They normally live in Long Lake as modern day woodsmen, like their father before them.

I myself have a five-foot, eight-inch frame and carry about twenty extra pounds in the middle. According to my driver's license, I have blue eyes and blonde hair, which, of course, are described as pale gray and medium-length dirty-blonde by my wife. I sit behind a computer most workdays for the past five years doing accounting for a law firm in Troy, New York.

We've been best friends since high school. I asked Peter and Mike to come on this camping trip because I needed only six more mountains to become a member of the Adirondack Forty-Sixers, an accomplishment they had already achieved. We had set up camp last night and climbed Phelps and Tabletop today. Tomorrow we are planning to climb Skylight and Mt. Marcy.

At our camp we relaxed and told stories of our past hiking trips. Some were of the marvelous places that we had visited in the Adirondacks; others were of places in the Northeast; and some were about the horror stories of just going out our backdoors for a quiet afternoon of walking in the woods. As I was wrapping up the tale of my first and last winter hiking experience in the southern part of the Adirondacks, a New York Department of Environmental Conservation Ranger entered our campsite with flashlight in hand.

The ranger stood patiently until I wrapped up my story and said in a deep but pleasant voice, "Good evening, gentlemen. Just your friendly neighborhood Ranger Bob McGrath stopping by to see if everything is all right, and ensure that you're doing what should be done to protect the forest of New York State."

The ranger was in his fifties with a worn leathery face, ghostly sunken black eyes, and a handlebar mustache. He was wearing his olive-drab wool ranger uniform with his Stetson hat set securely on his silver hair. His ranger badge on his left breast reflected our headlamps like a beacon in the night.

With my headlamp, I helped the ranger look over our camping gear, tents, and registration tag. Peter and Mike chatted together about taking me hiking this winter. Overhearing their quiet conversation, I turned and said to them in a threatening way, "The only way I'll go out hiking again in the winter is when hell freezes over."

Pete looked at Mike and replied sarcastically, "That happens lots around here, so I guess he's going with us."

Mike looked at me and said with an apologetic look, "You know, crossing four ice-covered streams and then breaking through two of them is not really normal for winter hiking, trust me. It was a fluke."

During that infamous hike, my borrowed snow-shoe straps broke, and I had to hike out in knee-deep snow. I got frostbite on my feet and a slight case of hypothermia from falling into the streams. Luckily, I made my way out of the woods with the help of a former hiking partner who I have never gone hiking with since. He calls me sometimes and asks if I want to go, but I always have an excuse for him, like a pulled muscle or some work to be done around the house.

"Well, everything is in order," Ranger McGrath said, "So, good night, gentlemen, and have a good hike come morning." He turned toward the trail to visit the next campsite up the way.

Before the ranger took a step away, Pete piped up, "Excuse me, can I get you to help us for a second? Would one bad experience keep you from going hiking again?"

The ranger came back into the light and stood silent for a few seconds. "Well, considering what I've overheard from your story, I think that it could have been worse. He could've had his hands or toes amputated, died of exposure, or fallen through and been frozen into the ice, only to be walked out in the spring. I always consider a person lucky when they walk out alive and are not dragged out in a body bag."

"What?!?" questioned Mike. "What do you mean frozen and walked out in the spring? That's impossible. A person could only survive maybe ten minutes in icy water."

Ranger McGrath stood a little taller and waved his flashlight over to an empty block of wood next to me and asked, "Do you mind if I sit down and tell you a story?" We all nodded, as we anticipated a storyteller's tale.

He pulled on his pant legs, sat on the block, and placed his flashlight next to him on the ground. With a deep cough he cleared his throat, looked us straight in our eyes, and said, "This story was told to me by another ranger about ten years back. On the coldest night that anybody could remember, something like fifty below, a twenty-one-year-old kid named Bobby closed a local bar in Saranac Lake. He staggered home and decided to take a shortcut across the northwestern end of the Oseetah Lake near Route 3. Well, the lake had just frozen over the previous week, so he gingerly tested the ice next to shore. And when it did not break, he proceeded to walk across. Because of the extreme cold, the lake was popping like crazy, like shotgun blasts echoing across the lake. The kid was so plastered and bundled up, he quickly got too hot and removed his clothes. He stripped down to only his boots and long johns and continued crossing the frozen lake without a care in the world. He took one step on a weak section of ice and fell through to the icy water of the lake."

I thought back on my own incident of falling through the ice. A cold shiver ran down my spine as I remembered the feeling of ice water soaking my pants and boots, how the clothes stiffened, and I immediately lost the feeling in my toes. I remembered how sleepy I became as

I desperately crawled my way to the car. I pushed on by saying that I would rest a hundred yards away. When I got there, I didn't stop but found a spot another hundred yards away. My former hiking partner pushed me to keep going. We got to my car, and he drove me to the local hospital.

The ranger's story continued, "Well, the kid didn't know which way was up and tried to swim to the surface, but before he could, the lake refroze." The ranger's voice went to a quieter and sadder tone. "He quickly lost all feeling in his body and continued to get sleepier and sleepier as his heart slowed. Bobby struggled to the ceiling of the lake on his last breath of air. He could hear his heartbeat, like a cannon firing, slowing as he struggled to stay alive." Then he took a long pause. "Thump..."

Mike, looking very confused, interrupted the old ranger's story, "This is about a drunk that... "

Quickly cutting Mike off, Pete said, "Dude, let him finish up!"

The ranger waited a moment before continuing. "The next morning a local police officer spotted the kid's clothes on the lake and called in the fire and rescue departments. They carefully followed the boy's tracks to the spot where they presumed he fell in. The officials continued the onshore search. The divers didn't find the kid under the ice, and that night the search was called off until something new turned up.

"That winter broke all the records, and with the thaw, even the winter diehards embraced the warmth of the spring. One rainy spring night the ranger who told me this story was in the same bar the kid had closed five months prior. Well, just before closing, the door opened, and there stood a drenched rat in a pair of boots and long johns. He quickly walked over to the bar and sat down, with water pooling on the floor. The bartender came over and asked him, `What would you like to drink, son?' The drenched rat replied, `W-W-Water, NO ICE!' The bartender got his drink. `Do you know h-h-how hard it is to s-s-sip water when you've been frozen in a g-g-goddamn block of ice for over f-f-five months?' yelled the drenched rat."

"The bar became deathly silent, and everyone looked at the newcomer. The ranger who was telling the story had been sitting next to the drenched rat. He looked at the memorial picture of Bobby, and his jaw dropped. After a moment of silence, he said, `Where in the hell have you been? The entire town has been looking for you; we thought you had drowned in Oseetah Lake.'"

"Bobby replied with a grin, `I-I-I told you I-I-I was f-f-frozen into the l-l-lake for the past f-f-five months, and I f-f-finally thawed enough to s-s-swim to sh-sh-shore. N-N-Nothing was open except this p-p-place, and I-I-I need-ed a d-d-drink r-r-really b-b-badly.' The bartender handed Bobby a double scotch, and he replied, `I-I-I quit drinking that stuff five months ago.'"

"The ranger asked the kid, 'How could you have survived five months under the ice? That's impossible.'"

"Bobby looked the ranger square in the eyes and said, 'I f-f-fell through and b-b-before I could get to the s-s-surface the i-ice ref-f-formed. I c-c-couldn't get out. I stayed next to the i-i-ice as long as I could, but I guess I was c-c-cold enough that my f-f-fingers f-f-froze in the ice, and before I knew it, I was f-f-frozen c-c-completely in the ice. I d-d-don't remember much, I j-j-just could t-t-tell when it was d-d-day and night b-b-but not much else.'"

"You're full of shit, or you've been drinking," Peter said to the ranger after a moment of silence.

"I'm not full of shit, and I haven't touched a drop since that night," replied Ranger McGrath with deadpan stare at my fellow hiker. "And if you don't believe me, that's fine with me. Well, gentlemen, I must be leaving now, so if you'll excuse me, I'll be off."

The ranger quickly got up and headed toward the next campsite. I looked at my watch and said that it was getting late if we wanted to have an early start tomorrow.

The next morning we all awoke, had a quick break-fast, and had started to pack our daypacks, when anoth-er DEC Ranger showed up, asked us for our permit, and looked over our campsite.

As I showed the DEC Ranger our hiking permit, I told him, "This place must be strict. You're the second ranger in as many days."

The ranger look surprised, "Second ranger? We were all over on Giant last night pulling a body out of the woods. There shouldn't have been anyone near here last night, and we didn't get out of the woods until nearly mid-night. Do you remember who you talked with?"

I replied after some thought, "I think he said his name was Bob something or other. He had on a similar uniform, and I think he checked all the other campsites here at Marcy Dam."

"Was it Bob McGrath? Did he have a handlebar mustache?" asked the ranger.

"He did have a mustache," I replied with a nod.

"Did he tell you any stories?" asked the ranger with a questioning look on his face.

"Yes, he did, a pretty good one at that," I replied as I remembered the farfetched tale.

The ranger smiled as if he was lost in a daydream. After a moment he said, "Half the stories he told were so unbelievable." A momentary pause. "But the problem was that the other half were completely true." Shaking his head in disbelief. "God, the last time I saw him was at his retirement party, and he told some great whoppers." A pause. "And that was last November." Another pause. "That was the last time I saw him, that is, until last night when we brought his body down off of Giant." The ranger turned and headed back over the dam to the rangers' cabin as he added his final thought, "Have a good day, gentlemen."

[Author Biography]

Ryan F. Schmit was born in Walton, New York and raised in Gouverneur, New York. He developed his love of the outdoors while growing up and exploring the beautiful Adirondacks. He attended SUNY Morrisville, where he earned AAS in Engineering Science. He attended Clarkson University, earning a BS in Aeronautical Engineering, and continued on to earn his MS and PhD. in Mechanical Engineering. For the past seven years he has worked in the Air Vehicle Directorate within the Air Force Research Laboratory at Wright-Patterson Air Force Base in Ohio. He is married to his loving wife of five years, Amy, and they have two sons together. Evan was born 15 weeks prematurely and passed away after two days of life. Aiden was recently adopted.